I stared at the dead body on top of my car.
I stared at the other two on the garage floor.

Then I stared at my husband. He was smiling at me. *Smiling* even though we had just bumped our formerly human, currently zombie killing spree total up to a nice round six (not counting Mack, since we didn't actually know if we'd killed him when he flew off my car in the parking complex).

"What?" I asked, because Dave's smile had gotten wider. "Why are you looking at me that way?"

He shrugged as he moved around toward the driver's seat. Before he got in, he grabbed the car zombie's ankle and yanked him off the roof with a violent tug. I heard him hit the ground below with a wet and somehow also crunchy *smack*.

"Nothing," Dave said with a shrug as he stood at the driver's side door. "I was just thinking how much cooler you are than any other girl I ever knew."

BY JESSE PETERSEN

LIVING WITH THE DEAD

Married with Zombies
Flip this Zombie

For Miriam and Michael,
without whom I might have just given up entirely.

CHAPTER 1

The Couple Who Slays Together...

David and I became warriors in the zombie plague on the first day, but don't think that means we were front line soldiers or something. In truth we stumbled into the zombie battle because it was a means for pure, physical survival.

But I never would have guessed that unlike therapy, unlike the self-help books that littered our apartment at the time, killing zombies would save my relationship.

But let me back up. It all started on August 10, 2010. Wednesday was couples therapy day. It had been for six months, although I was beginning to think that all this talking and sharing and role-playing that our therapist Dr. Kelly preached was nothing but a bunch of bullshit.

Despite her advice, despite all our visits to her office, David and I were on the brink. I had even researched divorce lawyers in our area on the Internet. The thing was, when I put "divorce lawyer" into the search engine on our shared computer...well, let's just say that I didn't have to type the whole phrase before it popped up in the system memory as something that had been searched for before.

So by the time we were driving down I-5 South into the heart of downtown Seattle toward Dr. Erica Kelly's tidy, sterile little office, I was just going through the motions of therapy and making a mental list of all the things I didn't like anymore about my husband.

The item I added to my list on August 10th was the CDs. You see, we share the car and the deal we'd struck was that since six CDs can fit into the changer, I could pick three and he could pick three. But as I cycled through the changer, keeping one eye on the road ahead of me, I realized that every CD was his.

Every. Fucking. CD.

That probably seems like a little thing, and in retrospect it was. But I guess that just goes to show you how far off the track we'd gotten.

I switched the stereo off with a flick of my wrist and glared at David from the corner of my eye. As usual, he was so wrapped up in one of those handheld games he loved that he didn't even notice my annoyance. Or maybe he was so used to it, he didn't care anymore. Either way, it sucked.

"Traffic seems pretty light," he said without looking up.

I glided onto the off-ramp and looked around. As much as I hated to admit it at that point, he was right. We'd lived in Seattle since our marriage five years ago and traffic was one of the main things that drove me nuts about the city. At any time of day or night there seemed to be thousands of cars crowding the highways. Sometimes I wondered where the hell they all came from.

But today, at four-thirty in the afternoon, when there should have been bumper-to-bumper cars and trucks honking their horns and blocking the street, instead there were no more than a handful of vehicles around.

I shrugged as I stopped at the red at the bottom of the ramp and checked to my left before I started to roll out into the intersection to make a right. Just as I touched the gas, an ambulance screamed by. I slammed on the brake with a gasp and barely avoided getting t-boned, first by the veering ambulance and then by the five police cars that raced behind it.

"Shit, Sarah," David barked, bracing himself on the dash of the car as he glared at me. His seatbelt strained against his shoulder. "Watch yourself."

"You know, if you're going to drive, maybe you should sit in my seat," I snapped, though I couldn't really blame him for being freaked out. I don't think I'd ever come so close to having a major accident and my heart was pounding. Without saying another word, I waited for the green before I double-checked for cars and made my turn.

Within a few blocks we pulled into the parking garage at the downtown office building we had been going to once a week since February. I sighed as I slid up to the guard box to check in and get our parking pass. But as I came to a stop, I realized that Mack, the usual security guy who greeted us every week, wasn't at his station.

You may think it's weird that I remembered his name, but I have a reason. You see, every time he checked us in, he asked who we were seeing, and when we said Dr. Kelly he gave us *the look*. The pity look. It stands out in your mind when a perfect stranger is giving you a "your relationship is doomed, how sad" face once a week.

When there wasn't the usual banter with the security guard, David looked up. "Not there, huh? Weird."

I glanced at him quickly then back to the empty box. "He must be around here somewhere. His TV is on, I can see the light of it flickering below the window line."

"Maybe he just went to take a leak or something," David said with a shrug. "Look, let's just park. We'll only be here a bit over an hour. If we have a ticket on the car when we come out, we'll go talk to him about it. He'll remember us. I'm sure we can work it out."

I stared again at the empty booth and gave a shiver. It just seemed so weird that after twenty-four visits with the same routine, today was suddenly different.

"You're right," I said as I put the car in gear and inched into the garage.

David let out a snort as he pocketed his game system in his hoodie and unbuckled his seatbelt. "Wow, I hardly ever hear *that*."

I swung the car into a space close to the elevator bank and slammed on the brake, purposefully making David catch himself on the dash a second time.

"Nice," he muttered with a glare in my direction as he got out.

So what I did wasn't subtle, but I couldn't help but smile as I followed him across the quiet parking complex to the elevator. It took a minute for the elevator to come and since we apparently had nothing to say to each other, we just stood there with the sounds of the streets outside the garage echoing around us as the only accompaniment to our dysfunction.

There were cars honking, sirens wailing, even the drone of a helicopter as it swooped in low overhead. I hardly noticed any of them. Now I kinda wish I had, though I don't know if I ever could have put two and two together at that moment. At that moment, it was just city noise, only magnified to the nth degree.

Once the elevator finally came, we rode up in silence, not even standing close to each other until the car dinged and came to a stop at the fourteenth floor of the complex. This ritual was so commonplace to us by now that neither of us needed to even look where we were going to find Dr. Kelly's office.

DR. ERICA KELLY, MS PSYCHOTHERAPY, MARRIAGE AND FAMILY COUNSELING.

I hated how the little letters etched on her door were so even. I can't even draw a straight line. The letters were a damned judgment.

The office was quiet as we stepped inside. Dr. Kelly had once rambled on and on about creating a calming "Zen" environment. I had only *just* kept myself from asking her if she wanted "Zen," why did she pipe in muzak versions of Nirvana songs that made my music-loving heart stop and my stomach turn every time? Today, though, the muzak wasn't a good band. I think it was Miley Cyrus, which was probably worse.

I turned toward the sliding glass area where Dr. Kelly's receptionist, Candy, generally sat. But, just like in the garage, the enclosed area was empty, though her little rolling chair had a pink sweater draped across the back of it and a half-drunk bottle of Diet Coke sat on the table top.

"Hey, Candy?" I called into the back office area as Dave flopped into a cushioned chair. "You here?"

There was no answer, so I signed the sheet that sat on the counter. It had a smiley face in the corner and Dr. Kelly's name and credentials in pretty lettering across the top. I wondered if they'd notice if I drew devil's horns on smiley? If Candy did, I guessed I'd have to explain myself to Dr. Kelly. I wasn't really in the mood to discuss which of my *feelings* had inspired me to be so naughty, so I fought the urge and set the pen down.

With a sigh, I took a place next to Dave. The couch was uncomfortable.

"What is up with everyone today?" I asked as I grabbed for a *Cosmo* magazine with the article title, "Please Your Man—In Bed and Out!" emblazoned across it. I didn't flip to it, but went straight for the horoscopes in the back.

"Just chill, Sarah," Dave said as he pulled his game out of his pocket. It lit up as he opened the case. "I'm sure she'll be back in a second."

"Yeah, I guess," I said as I looked at the empty vestibule a second time.

"So were the Wonderful Wilsons signed in?" Dave asked in a sing-song voice.

I let out an involuntary groan. The Wilsons. They were the couple who had the appointment right before ours. God knew why, seriously. They totally held hands on the way out, making little coo noises at each other. It was borderline disgusting.

Once I'd asked Dr. Kelly why the fuck they came to

therapy and she had tilted her head in that "how-do-you-feel-about-it-Sarah" fashion that made her perfect blond hair swing prettily around her heart-shaped face. Her smile was so calm it kind of made me want to punch her. Hard. Twice.

Then she said, "They come here for maintenance. Don't worry, Sarah, we'll get you and David there."

Maintenance. Like we were a car. Oh yeah, except that since I was spending a hundred and fifty dollars a week on a therapist, I couldn't afford the maintenance for my car and now it made this weird *clunk* sound whenever I turned left.

I glared at the clock. It was almost five now and Candy still wasn't at her desk.

"Do you think Candy Cane quit?" I asked in a hushed tone.

Dave laughed without looking up. I mean, really, who named their kid Candy and didn't expect people to crack *that* joke? I think it was her whole name, too, not short for Candace or anything reasonable like that.

"Okay, it's after five," I said as I watched the minute hand slip past the twelve.

"One minute." He looked up briefly. "Maybe the Wonderful Wilsons actually had a problem to discuss today. Do you really want to derail their perfect existence?"

"Their problem is that stick up their asses," I said as I tossed the magazine aside and got to my feet. "And now it's *two* minutes, Dave. Didn't Dr. Kelly lecture us about punctuality and how it equates to respect?"

"God, you are obsessive," he said as he snapped the game system shut and pocketed it. "Do you want to barge in there and demand two minutes' worth of cash from the woman?"

I stared at him, looking up at me from his slouched position on the couch. Sometimes I caught myself and remembered why I had liked him when I met him. Even now he looked...*bad*. You know, in a good way. Just a little tousled, just a *little* imperfect. Sort of sexy.

But then he glared at me and the moment passed, so I went back to cataloguing his faults, instead. *Unsupportive*, I added to myself.

"Yes. I do. *I'm* paying for this shit—" I ignored his flinching reaction to that. "—so I want my full benefit of it," I said as I pulled the door to the back room open and moved down the hall to the suite where we always met with Dr. Kelly. "Two minutes of money at a hundred fifty an hour can buy me—"

"A bottle of water and pretty much nothing else," Dave snapped as he followed me. "Come on, Sarah. There's no reason to be such a bitch."

"I can't believe you just called me a bitch!" I said, staring at him over my shoulder as I yanked the door open. "Dr. Kelly, do you approve of my husband calling me a—"

I turned toward the open office and stopped talking. There was our therapist of six months, wearing one of her impeccable black pantsuits with the usual silk shell underneath. This one was a bright blue that matched the pretty necklace dangling around her neck. And she was with the Wonderful Wilsons, just as we had suspected.

Only instead of sitting behind her desk with her notebook, looking over the rims of glasses I was sure were fake as she counseled the couple, Dr. Kelly was kneeling on the floor, her suit covered in blood. Mrs. Wilson, I think her first name was Wendie (with an "ie"), was sprawled out beside her with her throat still leaking blood from a huge bite on her neck. Her eyes were cloudy and blank.

As for Mr. Wilson…maybe it was Mark, I couldn't really remember….Well, Dr. Kelly was paying special attention to him. She had his limp hand in hers as she leaned over him…eating great hunks of flesh from his shoulder.

CHAPTER 2

Balance the workload in your relationship.
No one person should be responsible for killing
all the zombies.

I stared at Dr. Kelly, too stunned to fully comprehend that our Pacific Lutheran University-educated therapist was in the process of *eating* one of her couples. She did it with verve, too, something I wouldn't have guessed given the fact that I'd always thought the skinny little twerp was anorexic. But apparently what she needed wasn't a sandwich, as I'd often muttered as we left her office, but a *manwich*.

Yeah, David hadn't laughed at that joke when I told him later, either. But what can you do? In these situations you laugh or cry, right?

That day, I did neither, I just kept staring at the unreal picture in front of me. I guess part of me thought that if I looked long enough, this madness would somehow come into focus and have a logical explanation. Like maybe this was an experimental therapy. Or a joke?

Anything?

"What the fuck?" David said, his voice barely above a

whisper as he stared over my shoulder toward Dr. Kelly and the...well, the Less Than Wonderful Wilsons.

His voice drew Dr. Kelly's attention. She looked up from Mr. Wilson's neck, where she had begun gnawing with a stomach-churning set of crunches and wet smacks.

The first thing I noticed was that Dr. Kelly's eyes were no longer blue. Now they were red with huge pupils that didn't seem to focus on anything in particular, even when she looked right at us.

Her skin was a grayish tone, sickly and pale and...dead-looking, honestly. Except for her mouth, which was covered with a black substance that clung to her lips and teeth. Her chin was bright red with blood and sticky with flesh from the fresh meal she had just devoured.

"Um, Dr. Kelly," I said, hardly able to breathe. "Dr. Kelly, are you okay?"

She made a low, ugly growl, something that sounded more like a rabid dog than a human and then she lurched to her feet. When she turned slightly, I saw that the left arm of her suit jacket was torn, revealing a fresh wound of her own between her elbow and shoulder.

Blood was caked around the yawning hole, which revealed the bands of muscle beneath her skin, and my stomach turned as the shock began to wear off and the reality of our situation hit home.

"Sarah," David said from behind me, but his voice sounded weird and almost faraway because I was so focused on the woman before me.

Dr. Kelly lurched forward a step, then she twisted her head at the oddest angle and sniffed the air like a dog.

"Sarah," he said, this time louder.

I just couldn't stop looking at her, almost mesmerized by the way she stared at me with those weird eyes. Then she smiled, blood dripping from her lips.

"Sarah!" Dave yelled my name this time and I flinched as his voice echoed in my ears.

"What?" I screamed.

"Move!" he shouted, pushing me aside just as Dr. Kelly made a guttural cry and staggered toward me with remarkable speed for a woman in four inch peep-toe heels.

I fell across one of the couches in the room and flipped around just in time to see Dr. Kelly slam into David with her full body weight. He staggered into the hallway, holding her by the shoulders in an attempt to keep her off of him.

She swung her arms wildly, her perfectly manicured, pink nails slashing and her bloody mouth biting and twisting as she made every effort to get closer to him. The black bile substance leaked from her lips as she hollered and spit, spraying the stuff across her chest and onto David's previously white T-shirt.

"David!" I screamed, snapping out of my stunned disbelief as I watched my husband of five years fight for his life against what appeared to be a rabid marriage counselor.

"Sarah, a little help!" he grunted, pushing back against her with all his might.

And Dave isn't a tiny guy, either. He's just about six feet and playing video games all day instead of working has given him a bit of a tummy. The fact that he had to work so hard against five foot two and maybe a hundred pounds was terrifying.

I stared around me, looking for something to hit her

with, but the couches in the room were too big for me to lift and her chair was huge.

"I'm looking!" I cried as I moved to her desk. Her laptop was ultra-light, her books mainly trade-sized paperbacks with no sharp edges.

"Fuck, she's strong," David gurgled from the hallway.

"She does Pilates, I think," I said as I ripped a desk drawer open.

Inside, a letter opener glittered up at me. I rolled my eyes as I realized the handle was printed with the words, "Dr. Erica Kelly, MS Psychotherapy, Marriage and Family Counseling."

I had to give it to the woman, she knew how to advertise.

I grabbed for it and launched myself over the desk. Screaming like I was in a scene from *Braveheart*, I ran for her and thrust the letter opener deep into her back. It went in way easier than I expected and immediately black shit began to ooze out around the wound. With a yelp of disgust and surprise, I let go and backed up.

Dr. Kelly let out a growling cry and released David, only to turn toward me. The letter opener stuck out of her back like the hilt of a knife, its happy gold lettering glinting in the overhead fluorescent lighting (so much for Zen). As I realized she intended to attack me next, I reached for the opener, but she was already on me.

We fell backward, sprawling across the floor together. I pressed my hands against her shoulders just as David had, but she leaned into me with all her weight. It was like dead weight, too, extra heavy, and I wasn't nearly as strong as David. Her snapping jaws lowered, biting, always biting as she got closer and closer.

"David!" I grunted.

"I know," he yelled as he grabbed for the doctor's hair and pulled with all his might.

A chunk of blond softness yanked free, along with a bit of rotting scalp. David staggered back in surprise that her hair offered no resistance and hit the wall behind him, but Dr. Kelly didn't even seem to register what had happened beyond an annoyed grunt followed by more snapping jaws that I barely dodged by turning my head from side to side.

"Her shoe, David!" I cried. "Use her stiletto!"

As I somehow evaded more bites, I tried to look around Dr. Kelly toward David. He grabbed for one of her flailing feet and tore her shoe off. In that supremely crazy moment, I noticed her pedicure matched her finger-nails. I guess that's what my money went to.

Maintenance.

But I quickly forgot that when Dave came down next to us on his knees, raised the stiletto over his head, and slammed it down.

The heel entered Dr. Kelly's skull with a sickening crunch and then a wet sound I tried to pretend I hadn't heard. David pulled it free and little chunks of hair, scalp, and what I realized were brains flicked down on my chest and hands. I arched my back and turned my head to keep my face free of the disgusting rain.

He slammed the shoe down again, then a third time. He just kept swinging, pummeling our therapist until she made one last whining grunt and collapsed on top of me.

For a moment, actually probably a lot longer than a moment, we both were silent and still. He stared at Dr. Kelly, I stared at the bloody shoe in his hand. Then I squirmed beneath the weight of her now lifeless body.

"Get her off, David, please get her off!" I whispered.

With a grunt, he pushed her and she flipped away from me. As she flopped onto her back I heard the snap as the letter opener handle broke off against the floor.

I was on my feet instantly, brushing at my once favorite work blouse like somehow I could wipe away what had just happened. I'd gotten the shirt on a deep clearance at Nordstrom, so it was pretty and well-made. I always got compliments on it at the office.

But now it was ruined. The white was stained with blood, brain matter, and that black sticky substance that had drained from Dr. Kelly's mouth as she tried to eat me.

My stomach finally won in the war I'd been waging with it and I turned my head and vomited on the very couch where Dave and I had tried, rather unsuccessfully thus far, to save our marriage. I leaned over the arm for a long time, fighting dry heaves as I stared at my puke as it was slowly absorbed by the cushion.

Weird. The color of the two was almost the same, a gross, thin yellow.

Finally I straightened up and turned toward Dave. I found him staring down at what was left of the Wonderful Wilsons, half-eaten on the floor. Dr. Kelly's stiletto was still dangling from his bloody hand.

As I looked at him, my shock wore off enough that I could finally speak.

"Fuck me, David! Dr. Kelly just tried to eat us! Did that really happen? What the hell?" I shouted, my voice shaking, my hands shaking, my entire being shaking as hard as I had ever shaken before.

He turned toward me, the shoe in his hand slipping

free and clattering against the floor. It left behind a bloody shoe print on the pale carpet.

"I have no idea *what* that was," he said as he pulled his stare away from the dead bodies and back toward me. "She must have gone totally crazy. Like Jeffrey Dahmer-style or something."

"We checked her references, right?" I asked, looking down at Dr. Kelly. Her head was half caved in on the floor in front of us.

"Are you asking if I *knew* she was a cannibal psychopath, Sarah, but got lazy and just set up appointments with her for six Goddamn months anyway?"

Dave wiped his hands on his shirt as he spoke, but it did no good. The bright red blood only smeared on his skin and absorbed into the already messy cotton, turning the vintage t-shirt a weird, splotchy pink.

I stared at him and for the first time I noticed he was shaking as hard as I was.

"I don't know what I'm asking," I said, softening my tone as best I could. "I'm just trying to figure out what the hell happened. And what to do next."

He shook his head. "We call 911, *that's* what we do next. Though I don't know how the hell we're going to explain this to any normal person in the fucking universe. We just have to be honest. I mean, it was self-defense, right?"

I looked at him and drew back in shock. Oh hell, I hadn't even thought of that. What if the cops didn't believe us and we ended up in jail for murder?

"It was self-defense," I said with more decisiveness than I felt. After all, we'd never killed anyone before. "We'll just tell the truth and they'll have to see we had no choice but to fight her off."

I looked at all the bodies scattered about the room. I just hoped they wouldn't think we'd taken out the Wilsons, too. What was the threshold of kills to be classified as serial killers and mass murderers? I had seen it once on TV, but couldn't remember.

"They'll *have* to understand we had to do it," I whispered.

Dave reached for Dr. Kelly's office phone, which had somehow remained undisturbed on her desk despite the struggle, but just as his fingers closed around the receiver, the door to the adjoining bathroom that was in the corner of the room flew open.

Standing in the doorway, her breathing loud and wet through her bloodied nose and mouth, stood Receptionist Candy. She was dressed in a pink wrap dress that now gaped in the front, revealing an ample portion of what was apparently a fake tit. I knew it was fake because saline leaked from the huge gash that had been cut across the perky skin. The ragged edges, rimmed with black, told me the story before she even moved forward in a menacing fashion that almost perfectly matched Dr. Kelly's odd, jerking movements from earlier.

"Holy fuck!" David cried as he backed away, leaving the phone receiver to dangle from the desk. The sound of the dial tone pierced the air around us with a constant *beep, beep, beep* that was now our horror movie soundtrack. At least it was better than Muzak Miley.

Candy stumbled into the room, her gray mouth working and spewing black sludge just like Dr. Kelly's had. Blood stained her chin, her hands, even her clawing fake fingernails as she moved toward us.

"What the hell?" I screamed as I grabbed for Dave's shoulder.

More moans echoed to our right and both of us swung our gazes toward the sound.

The Wonderful Wilsons were starting to get up, first Mrs. Wilson with her slashed, chewed throat that dripped blood and then Mr. Wilson, who didn't seem to notice that Dr. Kelly had all but gnawed off his right arm, which now dangled by just a little bit of sinew and shattered bone.

"Run, Sarah," David said as he grabbed my hand and made for the door. "Fucking run!"

CHAPTER 3

Put the small stuff into perspective.
It's better to be wrong and alive than right
but eating brains.

We sat in the car with the doors locked, the panting noise of our matching breathing the only sound either of us made for a long time.

"We should turn on the car so we can listen to the radio and see if there are any bulletins," David said beside me. "I'm starting to think this might not be an isolated incident."

I nodded but when I lifted the keys to the ignition I couldn't fit them in the hole because I was shaking so hard. I tried once, twice, and finally David caught my fingers and helped me guide the keys into place.

"Thanks," I whispered without looking at him as I turned my wrist and the car roared to life.

He reached out to turn on the stereo and we were greeted by the sounds of the CD in the player. My annoyance, forgotten for a while, returned tenfold.

"Jesus David, fucking Whitesnake," I snapped as I turned in my seat to glare at him. "Who listens to that eighties-butt-rock shit anymore, let alone buys it in *CD* format? You realize you actually had to go out into the world and spend money on this, right?"

"I *like* Whitesnake," he said, and his angry expression probably matched my own pretty fucking well. "It's not like I kept my taste in music a secret from you when we got married. It's not like—"

"Oh no, you're right! You didn't have *any* secrets when we got married, did you? You were totally honest and look how well it's worked out." I interrupted with a wave of my hands. "I mean you told me you wanted to work in the finance industry... oh wait, you bailed on that, didn't you? You told me I could go back to school once you finished your MBA, but *no* you decided against that, too—"

"I'm not doing this right now. Put the car in drive," he snapped.

His tone pissed me off as much as the things I was saying to him did. I glared. "No. I think it's about fucking time we take Dr. Kelly's advice and talk this out."

"Dr. Kelly is dead! Her advice means shit now!" he shouted as he folded his arms.

"Just because she tried to eat us doesn't mean she was wrong," I countered, even though I'd really been fighting her advice for months now... not that I was going to admit that to him or anything. "I mean, she made some very good points over the past few months about the—"

He looked past me and his eyes widened. "Drive, Sarah! Drive!!"

At first I figured he was just making that face to

distract me from the argument because Dave isn't about confrontation, but I turned to look over my shoulder anyway, if only to call his bluff.

Only for once it wasn't a bluff. Rushing through the garage toward our car was the missing security guard, Mack. At first I was relieved. I was pretty sure he had a taser, which was better than anything Dave and I were packing (I think I had some gum, he might have had a pocketknife, but I wasn't sure). We could just tell Mack what had happened, he could phone it in, we'd fill out some paperwork, and it would be fine.

Except the closer he got, the more I noticed he was lurching like something out of the "Thriller" video. His gray skin and bloody face were enough to show he had been stricken by whatever insanity had turned Dr. Kelly into a ravenous cannibal and her secretary and the Wonderful Wilsons into moaning monsters.

"Shit," I muttered as I threw the car into reverse and pressed the pedal to the floor.

As the vehicle squealed backward, Mack seemed to recognize, even in his disturbed state, that he was losing a potential meal. He sprinted forward in that awful heaving way and lunged at the car.

I flinched as he grabbed the edge where the windshield met the hood and clung there, his gnashing teeth snapping against the glass and then lower, where he began to gnaw the hard metal of the hood. Even when a few of them snapped off, leaving bloody shards in his grey gums, he continued chewing, like he wanted to eat the car...or eat *through it* to get to us.

"Go!" Dave cried, snapping me out of my horrified interest in Mack's dental health.

Somehow I managed to slam the car into drive and take off in a cloud of burning rubber toward the exit.

Mack was a big guy and it seemed like his weight was even more offset than it had been when he was normal, so as I careened around a corner and sped toward the gate to the outside streets, he slid.

His face was awful as it hit the front windshield, a twisted, pained mass of something inhuman. And yet I felt very little sympathy as I burst through the yellow gate arm and sent him flying off somewhere into the distance.

Slamming onto the city streets, both David and I sucked in deep breaths of relief. He pushed a button and got the stereo off the CD and back to the FM station. Just as we'd hoped, the emergency three-beep system was in effect, something instituted after 9-11 to give out info in an emergency.

Beep, beep, beep, then a pause before the facts we so desperately needed piped through the crappy speakers.

"Good afternoon," came a flat, female voice that sounded like it had been fed plenty of Prozac. "Your attention, please. There has been a chemical or biological emergency. Please stay in your homes with the doors and windows locked until further instructions become available. Only call 911 in a true emergency."

We held our collective breath but instead of elaborating, the system clicked back into three beeps and then the same message repeated. David hit the stereo power button hard enough that it snapped off and rolled under my seat. At least the annoying repetition ended.

"Great. One more thing broken," I muttered. He

opened his mouth to argue but I shook my head. "It's the least of our problems."

"They said biological or chemical," he said as he rested his head back against the car seat and stared at nothing in particular. "I hope whatever's causing this isn't floating around in the air."

I nodded but didn't answer because the thought of what David said made my skin crawl and my blood grow cold. Watching someone we knew turn into a raving lunatic willing to kill and eat another person was bad enough, but what would it be like to know it was happening to you?

"Okay, we need a game plan," I said as I moved up the freeway ramp going north toward our apartment. "What do we do now?"

David stared at the stereo display, dark now after his tantrum. "We go home."

I glanced at him, able to do it while driving because for the first time in five years there wasn't any traffic to pay attention to during my merge.

"Go home?"

He nodded as he stared past me toward the cityscape, rising up beautifully with the sparkling waters of the Puget Sound behind it. It looked so peaceful. What a lie.

"That's what *they* say to do and I think it's our best option," he said. His voice sounded like he was numb. I was, too. "Actually, I think that's our only option for the moment."

I stared at him for a moment and then I nodded. "Okay, home it is."

We drove in silence, our normally forty-minute drive

made short by the lack of people on the street. Okay, that wasn't true. There were people on the street, but they were no longer driving or human. A few straggling...*things* like Dr. Kelly and Mack roamed the edge of the highway. Crashed cars littered the side of the street. In the median, we watched as two creatures gnawed on the legs of a highway patrol officer. Eventually David closed his eyes and I kept mine straight ahead on the road.

We'd seen enough, I guess.

Our apartment, just north of what they called the "U-District," was shitty. The cost of living in Seattle is fucking ridiculous and since David hadn't been working, at least in a traditional sense, we couldn't really afford something better.

Our neighborhood was dingy, old, and had its share of homeless druggies and girls who turned tricks in the alleys. But we *did* have the security of an underground garage, although after our last garage adventure...well, I don't think either of us felt safe as I rolled the window down and reached out to enter the code that sprung the gate open.

I snatched my hand back in and hit the window control in rapid succession so that it rolled up, then we moved into the gloomy garage. I parked in our assigned space and we glanced at each other before we each unlocked our doors and stepped out into the cool air of the underground facility.

A car alarm screamed in the distance. Normally I'd ignore it or just be annoyed by it, but today I looked toward the sound with a shiver. Car alarms took on a new meaning for a long time after the outbreak. I mean, *something* had to have set them off, right? But that day, in the misty dark of the industrial LED lights, I didn't see anything moving.

"Sarah, look," David said. He was motioning toward the elevator and his face was long and pale and sick.

I moved around the car toward him and instantly saw what he did. Another vehicle was smashed against the back wall nearby, its front end caved in and coolant fluid dripping into a greenish pool on the concrete floor.

"Isn't that Jack and Amanda's car?" I whispered, thinking about our next door neighbors.

They were about our age, and while I wouldn't call them friends we were cordial and had copies of each other's keys just in case we got locked out or needed someone to grab the mail during a vacation.

Sometimes the guys got together to play Xbox or something, normally when I worked late since I didn't care for Jack and his loud, obnoxious personality. He was a burper and farter... and he thought it was *hilarious*. Yeah, super classy guy.

"It looks like it," Dave said as he reached back and took my hand. "Come on."

After he pushed the 'up' button, the elevator seemed to take forever, but finally it opened with a *ding* that echoed in the garage. David peeked inside first and then pulled me in behind him. As I reached for the third floor button I noticed blood smeared across the number. With a little groan, I pulled my hand inside my sleeve before I pushed it.

Dave shook his head with a nervous laugh. "You've got it all over you now, I don't know how covering your hand can help at this point."

"Me neither, but I'd rather not rub it all over me

regardless," I said as I leaned back against the metal wall and folded my arms.

"Too late," he said, motioning behind me.

I straightened up and turned to see I'd leaned right into a large smear of black sludge like the kind the people around us were vomiting when they were...*infected* or whatever was happening to them.

"God. *God!!*" I said.

Okay, I whined it. Whatever, cut me some slack. All I wanted was a shower and to wake up from this disgusting dream and have everything just be *normal* again.

The door opened and like in the garage, Dave stepped out first. He looked around and then motioned me into the hall behind him as he dug for his house keys in his front pocket. With a few half-jogging steps, we reached our door. He let us in and immediately flipped the deadbolt behind him.

With a sigh of relief, both of us looked around our seven-hundred-square-foot apartment. I'd never loved the piece of shit more. Every problem we'd ever had with the place was forgotten in that instant and I wanted to get down on my knees and kiss the floor.

"You know what this is, right?" Dave said, his voice happily keeping me from making out with the linoleum square in front of our door.

I looked at him. "What?"

"Zombies."

He nodded as I stared at him with what I'm sure was an incredulous expression. He actually looked serious.

"You need to lay off the movies, dude," I snapped as I shook my head. "*Zombies?* That's the stupidest thing I've ever heard in my life."

"No it isn't!" He actually sounded offended that I'd doubt his brilliant deduction. "It makes sense. Or at least as much as anything can based on what happened to us today."

"David—" I drew his name out with frustrated annoyance.

He moved toward me with a frown. "Fuck, Sarah, our therapist tried to *eat* us. So did about ten other people since then. We saw things I never thought I'd see in my life. What else could it be but zombies?"

I stared. Apparently the stress of the day had broken my husband's brain or something. At the time I just couldn't accept that the stuff of cheesy movies was real.

"I can't talk to you when you're like this," I said, grabbing for the remote to turn on the television.

On the screen scenes of smoky downtown streets greeted us. I sighed in relief. At least it looked like the television was going to give us more information than the radio emergency broadcast had on the way home.

"Will you watch?" I asked as I tossed Dave the clicker. "I have to pee and I want to get out of these bloody clothes. Then you can change and I'll watch."

He grunted, his displeasure with my dismissal of his theory obvious as he took a seat on the couch. I gritted my teeth at the blood he smeared on the cushions when he flopped back, but decided against starting anything. I was too grimy and gross and uncomfortable for it. I'd just have to put Resolve on the cushions and scrub them while he changed later.

I walked to the bathroom and closed the door behind me. It was a cramped space so I edged in, dropped my slacks, and sat down on the toilet, only to sink into the water. With a yelp, I got back up and dragged a towel from the rack.

David had left the seat up... *again*.

I rubbed the water off my ass as I muttered a whole lot of choice names about the doofus out in the living room. As I turned to hang the towel back on the rack, I caught my reflection in the mirror behind me. With a groan, I leaned closer to the mirror to examine myself.

My hair, which is normally a light brown, was caked with blood so that it had a ruddy hue. To be honest, it wasn't a bad color for me. If we ever had money again, I figured maybe I'd dye it a similar shade.

The state of my outfit pissed me off more. My once-white shirt was smeared with sludge and dirt and brains. It was totally ruined. There was no way I was going to get dried blood out of white linen even if I pre-soaked from now to the end of time.

"Damn it," I muttered as I started to unbutton the blouse, but as I got to the second button, I froze. From behind the shower curtain came a faint but undeniable scraping noise.

I swallowed. Once again, the scraping echoed in the tiny room. There was definitely something behind the curtain. I prayed it was a cat that had gotten through the window. Or an opossum. A rat.

Anything but what I thought it was.

I grabbed for the closest thing there was to a weapon in the room: a hard-backed copy of one of the Dr. Phil love books. I'd given it to David when we started therapy months ago. It had sat on the back of the toilet tank ever since. I don't think he'd cracked it, which annoyed the hell out of me, but it was pretty heavy and had sharp corners, so I held it up as I grasped the edge of the shower curtain and threw it back.

Standing in the tub, staring at the tiled back wall as he swayed gently back and forth, was our neighbor, Jack. That's the guy whose car we'd seen in the garage earlier. He turned with sort of a sluggish boredom toward me and I suppressed a squeal of surprise.

Whatever biological or chemical *thing* had been released on our city had obviously affected him, too. His body, already hefty from eating too much junk food and playing too many video games, now leaned at a weird angle and his soft gray skin looked clammy.

He stared at me for what seemed like forever and then his mouth opened and he vomited sludge all over my green bathmat before he moved in my direction.

"Shit," I groaned. "Why couldn't you be a cat?"

I didn't wait for him to answer that rhetorical question. I swung my book and hit him square in the forehead. His rotting skin split, covering Dr. Phil's picture with a layer of gooey blood and chunks of flesh.

Jack blinked at me, almost like a confused gorilla in a zoo, and then continued to lurch toward me. Unfortunately... or I guess fortunately for me, he no longer had the wherewithal to step up and over the tub ledge. His legs caught on the smooth surface and he tottered off kilter and fell forward.

Out of pure instinct and a hefty dose of luck, I flattened against the back wall as his bulky body careened past me. His already shredded forehead hit the thin bottom seat of the toilet with a clang and he let out a whining groan.

I don't know what came over me as I looked down at our fat, piece of shit of a neighbor lying half in my toilet, the offending seat Dave had left for me still flipped up overhead. I certainly didn't think about what I was going to do, I just did it. Dropping down, I started slamming the toilet down against his skull.

"Put. The. Toilet. Seat. Down. David!" I accentuated each word with a crushing bang of the seat.

I didn't stop until I heard Dave's voice outside the door.

"Did you say my name?" he called from the hall, breaking me away from my furious spell and forcing me to stare down at the mess I'd made.

The toilet was cracked and covered in blood, along with brain matter, some loose flesh and I think part of an ear, although it was so mangled that I wasn't sure and I didn't want to lean closer and look.

Poor Jack was most definitely dead, his red eyes now dark and no longer clouded by a desire to eat me. Or at least the one still in his skull. I'd crushed the other one sometime during my tirade.

I stared down at the seat again. I still really had to pee. I mean, *bad*. See, when I get nervous, I have to go and honestly, was there anything to make you more nervous than being attacked by flesh-eating, infected humans?

I'd been holding it since we killed Dr. Kelly and now my bladder screamed at me. The apartment was a one bed, one bath so if I wanted to go…this was it.

And at that point, I have to tell you, bodily functions were starting to win out over being disgusted or disturbed by dead people on my floor. With a grunt, I shoved Jack's fat body out of the way. He hit the tile face down with a splat that sent droplets of all kinds of gross flying everywhere.

I flipped the upper toilet seat back into place. Although it wasn't covered in as much blood as the rest of the toilet, I didn't exactly want to sit on it, so I braced myself against the sink and the wall, sort of hanging over the seat as I took care of my business. I flushed, and to my surprise our toilet actually disposed of most of the body parts and blood without backing up. After a second courtesy flush, all evidence of the attack spun away to the sewer.

Well, except for the blood, brains, and body on my floor, of course.

With a grimace, I pulled my pants back up. In the small bathroom, Jack's dead body blocked most of the floor. Gingerly I stepped up onto his squishy, out-of-shape ass and balanced there as I washed my hands with steaming hot water and probably half the bottle of liquid soap. When I was finally satisfied that I'd cleansed myself, or at least my hands, of all my sins, I went back into the hall.

Dave was standing in the living room now, leaning over the back of the worn easy chair as he watched the TV screen. The speakers were turned up so loud that I guessed he hadn't heard my vicious clash in the bathroom.

At least I *hoped* he hadn't heard me battling against our neighbor and just left me to it while he checked out the sports scores which were still oddly scrolling along the bottom of the screen on the highlighted runner.

Hey, the Mariners won.

"Babe," I said, calling him by an endearment for the first time in so long I couldn't remember when.

He turned toward me with an expression of surprise, although I wasn't certain if it was because I called him *babe* or because I was covered in even more gore than I had been the last time he saw me moments before. I motioned toward the bathroom. He stepped closer and peered in at Dead Jack and then back toward me with wide eyes.

"I think you might be right after all," I said with a nod. "Zombies."

CHAPTER 4

Talk out your big decisions. Hear both opinions before you decide if you're going to flee the city or hole up with Campbell's Soup and CNN.

Dave continued to stare at the mangled body on the bathroom floor, which was pooling with blood and mung now.

"So you killed him with *what* now?"

"I tried that Dr. Phil book at first," I sighed as I looked at the offending tome, lying next to Jack's lifeless body, its pages caked with fluids and unidentifiable mush. "And I finished off with the toilet seat. Just so you know, you left it up again. That drives me crazy."

"Sorry," he said, his voice flat and emotionless.

He gave an absent nod as he pulled the door shut. It was weird how quickly all this was becoming normal, commonplace.

"Come on, we have to watch this," he said as he motioned to the television. "It's like all hell is breaking loose...*literally*."

I'm sort of sad to say that I pretty much instantly forgot about the man I'd just brutally killed in the bathroom. I moved to the couch with David and we sat close together on the edge of the cushions.

CNN was the station he'd chosen. An anchorman sat at the desk, his face long and serious as he spoke in that weird, droning voice that I guess they must teach them in journalism school.

"The outbreak is thought to have begun in a high-security laboratory housed on the University of Washington campus and has spread with enormous speed throughout the city. Attacks by the infected have been reported all across the greater Seattle area, which contains close to four million people. We go to local reporter Henry Greene for more."

The screen switched to another man in a bad suit who was standing near the famous Pike Place Market. Its iconic sign blinked as dusky darkness began to settle over the troubled city.

"Thanks, Roger," Reporter Henry Greene said as he looked straight into the camera without even blinking. "There are several reports I can update you on. First, there were rumors that one of the infected managed to board a flight to San Francisco. This *has* been confirmed by the FAA just in the last few moments. It seems that the plane is now running entirely on autopilot as the crew and the roster of passengers have apparently been stricken by this infection mid-air. The Pentagon is now debating whether to shoot it down over an area of low population rather than allow the flight to land as planned on its auto-nav system. We should have more on that developing situation within the hour."

"God," I whispered, trying hard not to think of those poor people trapped on the doomed flight.

I'd never really liked flying. That was the one bonus to barely scraping by, if we wanted to get somewhere, we drove or took the bus. Now I guess it was an even better idea. More room for escape in those modes of transportation.

"In addition, several fires have started in the downtown area and we have heard that..."

The reporter stopped as his never-wavering stare suddenly flicked away from the camera and instead moved off in the distance. His eyes widened slightly.

"Uh, Ken..." he said, clearly talking to a producer or the camera man. "Ken, do you hear that noise? What is th—oh my God!"

The camera spun and looked up the steep hill in the distance. The shaking lens was off focus for a minute, then it auto-corrected and both Dave and I gasped at once. There was a huge group of people standing at the top of the hill just a block from the market.

Okay, not people. Zombies. They were growling and lurching and that was the first time we ever saw them run in a herd. They rushed down toward the market en masse, their cries and grunts audible even from the distance.

"Christ, Henry, run!" the man behind the camera said, his voice muffled since the mike wasn't pointed toward his mouth.

The reporter was already a few strides in front of him, running toward the partly enclosed market. The camera bounced almost like it was shooting a really low-budget "handheld" horror movie as the cameraman followed, but before they'd gotten too far another mob of growling creatures began to flood from the open stalls in front of them, crowding toward the two men as sludge poured from their lips and bared teeth.

"Oh no—" the reporter whispered, his voice strangely soft and calm as he faced what could be nothing but his ultimate demise.

But then the voice cut away and the screen switched back to the CNN reporter at the anchor desk. He was now almost as gray as the zombies were and he stared at the camera with a disbelieving and utterly horrified expression.

I would assume that *wasn't* something they taught in journalism school.

"We—we've obviously had some technical difficulties, folks," he finally said as he shook himself awake from his stunned fog. "But I assure you we'll work to keep you updated on the situation with local coverage on the ground and try...well, we'll try to get back with Henry shortly."

Dave's eyebrows lifted with disbelief. "Yeah. Henry's a zombie, dude."

I nodded. "We now go to Zombie Reporter Henry Greene on the scene," I answered, mocking the CNN reporter's cadence. "Henry want brains."

Dave didn't laugh, but he smiled, which was about as good as it was going to get at this point. The reporter continued to drone on in the background, telling us all to stay in our homes and remain calm.

I shook my head at the idea of doing either of those things. "Did you hear what he said about Seattle?"

Dave rolled his eyes at me. "Um, that we're at the heart of a zombie plague. Yeah, Sarah, I got that."

"No," I snapped, irritated by his defensiveness. "I

meant what he said about how many people are in this area. Four million, David. *Four million* people."

He kept watching the screen, reminding me of so many times I'd tried to talk to him but his video game was more important. Or his show. Or whatever.

"So?" he said.

"*So!*" I repeated with a wave of my hands that finally got his attention again. "We've already seen how fast this *thing*, whatever it is, is spreading. Think about it... if it started at U-Dub sometime today, that's *miles* from where Dr. Kelly's office is... um, *was*."

He nodded. "I guess."

I continued without slowing down. "Hell, someone infected got all the way to Sea-Tac, through security and boarded a plane before anyone caught it, which probably means they were bitten right at or even *in* the airport which is what... twenty miles away from the university?"

Dave stopped giving me the look and nodded somberly. "I get what you're saying. It's spreading fast."

"I'm saying that this city is a buffet," I said as I got up and paced the small room. "If *they* don't get it under control, there are going to be more zombies than people in a pretty damn short amount of time."

David's focus shifted back to the television screen, where they were now showing footage taken from the ever-filming camera at the top of the tower in Red Square at the University of Washington. It was a steady shot, so it didn't pan as lurching zombies moved in and out of frame below. Occasionally an uninfected person ran through the scene, but he or she was almost always chased by an undead bastard or twenty.

"If we aren't outnumbered already," Dave whispered with a shiver. "Maybe staying here isn't such a hot idea."

I nodded. That had been my thought, too.

"Yeah, but that means going back out into the street," I whispered. "And facing...*them*. Lots of them. So if we decide to leave...then what do we do to keep from getting turned into zombies?"

He pulled his gaze from the screen. "Well, we've watched a lot of zombie flicks."

I arched a brow, a little action I'm pretty proud of perfecting since it took me months of practice. "Are you suggesting that we can battle real zombies with horror movie techniques?"

"Why not?" he asked with a shrug.

I rolled my eyes. "Yeah. This isn't that movie *Scream*."

He frowned, clearly annoyed once again by my lack of faith in his ideas. "Well, do you have a better idea? It's not like you can find out information about *real* zombies online. Anything anyone knows about this kind of stuff comes from watching movies or reading books on the subject. *Fiction* books, Sarah."

I opened and shut my mouth, unable to formulate any kind of response. Once again, to my great frustration, Dave was right. I mean, I couldn't think of one thing I knew about zombies that didn't come from movies.

We used to love those flicks, sitting together on the couch in the dark. Lately I hadn't been watching movies with him as much. With all our fighting and me working as much as I could to keep us financially afloat, it hadn't been a priority. But I guess I had just as good a grasp on the genre as anyone. And at least if we put together a list of what we knew it felt like we were *doing* something rather than just sitting around waiting for the National Guard to get their act together.

"Okay, so what do we know about zombies?" I finally sighed.

He grinned at my agreement to take part in this little exercise even though I still had serious doubts about it.

"Well, when someone is bitten, they turn into a zombie," he offered. "But it doesn't seem to be airborne or passed by any touch that doesn't break the flesh."

I shivered at the idea, still more terrifying than anything to me. "And we know that from personal experience, not just movies. So score one for *Dawn of the Dead*; they got that part right." I smiled though it didn't feel very strong. "Maybe this idea isn't so far off the mark after all."

"Gee, thanks," he said in a flat tone. "So what else? We know they want to feed on live people, but they don't seem to feed on other zombies. At least *we* haven't seen that."

"True, the Wonderful Wilsons and the zombies on the side of the road even worked together to feed." I was starting to get more into this little exercise and I started to wish I had a notebook to write it all down. "And we both saw the group that just got that poor reporter and his cameraman. They were almost like some kind of fucked up pack of animals from *Wild America* or something. But what about other animals? Or just meat like in a store? Would they eat stuff like that? Could an animal be turned into a zombie?"

Dave shrugged. "We don't know about that yet. I guess we just keep an eye out. If animals were infected...that could be bad. They can hide a lot better than a person."

I shut my eyes and tried not to think too hard about

Fluffy the Friendly Terrier or Ming the Cat becoming a killing machine. To keep my mind off the subject, I tried to pull together some more information to add to our running tally.

"It seems like a head injury stops them cold if it's bad enough. Like with the shoe in Dr. Kelly's head or the toilet seat and Jack."

"In the movies they have shotguns and other weapons," Dave said.

I nodded. That was very true. "Too bad we don't have anything like that, but I guess we could try to get them if we went out. I mean, sporting goods stores carry that stuff. We could break in or maybe we'll even find people hiding there to team up with."

He smiled. "We'll put it on the to do list."

I laughed because my 'to do' list is legendary around our house. I love crossing off the stuff I've done. It drives Dave crazy because he's much more fly by the seat of his pants.

Dr. Kelly once said we needed to find a way to respect our differences and use them to our advantage. Turns out we only needed to kill her in order to make that a reality. I wish we'd known that months and thousands of dollars ago.

"As far as weapons go, until we can find a place that carries guns and ammo, we can look around the house for stuff that might work. So far we've done pretty well with using what was available," I said.

"We have," he agreed. "That shoe idea in Dr. Kelly's office was pretty sharp. So was using the toilet seat on Jack."

I blushed. Dave hadn't complimented me in a long time and I felt positively girlish now. "Thanks."

"We should also see how much food we have that's

non-perishable and portable," he said. "Even if we decide not to go, but stay here for a while, we'll have to ration. And we should eat the perishable stuff first since we have no idea if we'll be losing power or something soon."

I swallowed hard. I hadn't thought about that, but it was a possibility. The government could shut the lights down if they got it in their heads. Or if there wasn't anyone left to mind the power plants... well, they'd shut *themselves* down at some point.

I'd learned that disturbing tidbit from the Discovery Channel, though, not zombie movies.

"I'll start the oven and cook a frozen pizza for dinner tonight. And I'll start sorting food and make a tally of what we have," I said, moving toward the kitchen. But before I'd gotten into the other room, there was a knock at the door.

Dave and I froze and I slowly turned back to face him. He stared at the door and then at me before he looked around the cramped living room for some kind of weapon. With a grin, he found the wooden baseball bat that had been propped up in the corner unused since Dave dropped out of graduate school and quit his school softball team.

I smiled at his choice. "Zombie movie classic," I whispered. "Nice."

I looked around for my own weapon and my gaze fell onto our wedding photo. It was a big one my Mom had insisted we buy from the photographer. An eleven by fourteen monstrosity of us standing in front of a church with rice scattering in front of us. We looked happy. We *were* happy.

I pulled the photo down and turned it so that a corner was ready to be used as a bludgeon.

"And once again, very creative," he encouraged.

I smiled, then cautiously moved toward the door.

The knock sounded again, this time louder.

"Dave? Sarah? It's Amanda!" came a voice from the hallway.

My mouth dropped open. I mean, I knew I'd had to kill Jack in the bathroom, but I hadn't really thought about facing his live-in girlfriend, Amanda, after I did it.

I moved on the door, but Dave grabbed my wrist. "Sarah, if Jack was a zombie, it follows that *she* might be bitten, too," he whispered in a harsh, low tone that hardly carried.

I jerked my hand away from the door and stared at it. He was right. I hadn't been thinking about my safety, just my rapidly increasing guilt.

"Please, if you're there let me in!" she said from the other side. I could hear she had been crying and was just barely holding it together now.

I inched forward and put my eye up to the peephole. Fuck, it was too hard to tell if she was infected. In the wavy image, I could see her clothing was caked with blood and her brown hair was falling out of its usually sleek ponytail. She'd clearly been through something, but both Dave and I were also coated in blood and we were still rational humans.

"Amanda, have you been bitten?" I asked, taking the risk of letting her know we were home and still had tasty brains for hungry zombies.

Dave slapped at my arm lightly, but I ignored him.

"*What?*" she sobbed. "Please, Jack went crazy and I crashed the car and cut my arm all up on the glass. I can't find him now and the TV is really freaking me out."

My heel bounced on the linoleum, a nervous habit of mine, as I stared out at her. She looked around the hall, huddled up as small as she could make herself. She looked scared, that was the one thing I could see for sure. The girl wasn't the brightest bulb and her taste in men sucked, but I still sort of liked her.

"Amanda, I'm going to open the door, but if you try to eat us, I'll fucking kill you."

"*What*?" her muffled voice elevated to a squeak on the other side of the door.

"Sarah," Dave sighed from behind me.

I turned on him. "I killed her boyfriend. I should at least let her in and we can see if she's...zombiefied or whatever."

He shrugged. "I guess we can manage to murder one more acquaintance if it comes to that."

I hoped it wouldn't as I slipped the lock free and opened the door.

CHAPTER 5

Don't discuss your relationship problems
with friends. Your zombie problems are
another story entirely.

Amanda fell into the apartment more then walked in as
the door opened, but her stumbling motion seemed too
smooth to mean she was a zombie. I think she was just
freaked out and seeing other people she knew gave her
permission to lose it a little.

As she sat on the linoleum square in front of our door
and sobbed, I nudged her feet out of the way and shut and
locked the door behind her.

Dave and I watched her from a safe distance. She was
crying so hard, I kind of wanted to comfort her, but I
didn't want to end up undead so I stayed near him, picture
frame at the ready, and Dave looked like he was about to
pop a fly ball over the wall at Safeco.

Once her tears subsided, Amanda looked up at us and
our positions and weapons seemed to register with her.
Her brow wrinkled with confusion.

"*What* is going on with you two?" she sniffled as she
moved to get up.

"Hey, just go slowly," Dave snapped as he lifted his bat in a menacing fashion.

Amanda's eyes widened but she slowed down as she pushed to her feet against the front door and stared at us. She was wearing a tank top and there was blood smeared both on it and on her arms.

Just like she'd said, I saw a small cut on her bicep, but it wasn't ragged or tinged with black sludge like the bite marks I'd seen on the other zombie victims. Her long cotton cargo pants covered her legs too much to say for sure about ankle nips, though.

"Can you roll your pant legs up to your knees so I can get a look?" I asked, feeling kind of like a cop checking for pot. "Slowly."

"Come on, you guys—" she started with a Valley Girl pose of annoyance.

"Just do it," Dave said. "We'll explain everything to you once we check you."

She was pissed, there was no denying that, but she bent over and pulled her pant legs up one after another. She had a stereotypical "pretty girl" tattoo of a daisy chain around her ankle, but no visible signs of a bite.

Dave lowered his bat carefully. "Okay, but we're going to keep an eye on you, so just stay back a bit."

She folded her arms. "Have you two gone nuts? You're talking about eating people, killing people, hitting me with a *bat*!"

"You can't be too careful with zombies roaming around, Amanda," I explained with a shrug.

"Zombies?" She stared at us with a blank expression that I'm sorry to say was pretty much normal for her. The lights had always been on with Amanda, but I'm not sure she was home much. "What are you talking about?"

Dave stared at her with an expression of both intense annoyance and utter shock. "I thought you said you were watching TV."

She shifted and her cheeks colored with pink embarrassment. "They were talking about chemicals and infections and I got confused and freaked out. I tried to find something else to watch, I mean tonight is supposed to be *American Idol*, but every channel is playing the same show, so I just turned it off."

Dave rolled his eyes and paced across the apartment. As much as I disliked Jack, David *hated* Amanda. He told me time and again that she was too stupid to be my friend. But she kind of reminded me of a cute puppy. You couldn't blame her for being dumb as a rock.

And that might be insulting to rocks.

"Okay, Amanda, let me give you the crib notes," I said with a sigh. Dave was going to be no help here. "Sometime earlier today something bad happened at U-Dub. Really bad. It turned a bunch of people into zombies."

"Like movie zombies?" she asked, blinking at me with empty disbelief.

"Exactly...." I looked at Dave and he shrugged. "Well, we *think* so, anyway. So far they seem to work the same way. Our marriage counselor tried to eat us and we killed her by bashing her head in. That's pretty much just like the movies, right?"

"Oh my God," Amanda said, reaching out to pat my arm awkwardly. Her eyes had filled with tears. "Marriage counseling? Are you guys okay?"

"I don't know," I found myself saying, too tired and weirded out to be guarded.

Dave moved toward us with a scowl. "Look, that's not the point. The point is that we got attacked by zombies in this therapist's office, later in the parking garage of her building, and then Sarah found a zombie in the bathroom here at our apartment."

I glared at him and he shut his mouth. I think he was so pissed about Amanda's cluelessness and maybe the fact that I'd just outed we were in counseling that he'd momentarily forgotten just *who* I'd bashed to death with a toilet.

We were all quiet for a minute and then I noticed Amanda's cuts were bleeding. The blood made weird little trails down her arm. It was gross, but at least it wasn't sludge.

"Let me get you a towel," I said.

At first I moved for the bathroom, but then I stopped. If I opened the door in there, Amanda would see Jack's body and I wanted to ask her some questions before I revealed anything so horrifying to her.

Checking myself, I went to the kitchen and grabbed a dish towel instead. I wet it lightly and brought it back out to Amanda.

She smiled as she took it and started wiping off her cut. As she carefully bound the wound, I decided to broach the subject of her dead boyfriend.

"So you said that Jack went crazy, right?" I asked as I motioned her toward a chair. "What happened exactly?"

Her makeshift bandage secure, Amanda nodded, sniffling as she took a place on the chair. I found a box of tissues and handed her a few. She wiped her eyes as she spoke, streaking mascara across her face until she looked like a Disney-animated raccoon.

Raccoons carried rabies, right?

"Okay, so we went to the Gas Guzzler right up the street," she began. "Jack had been drinking and wanted more beer, so I drove."

I rolled my eyes. How charming on a Wednesday afternoon when the rest of the world was working or spending time with their family . . . or killing their zombie therapist across town.

Not surprisingly, Amanda didn't seem to notice my reaction to the beginning of her story.

"I stayed in the car while he went inside. He was in there for a while and when he came back he was all upset. He said some homeless freak bit him and then went over the counter at the clerk."

I shut my eyes for a minute as I pictured Jack's red eyes and his black mouth before he tried to get to my brains in the bathroom.

"I wanted to call 911 and take him over to the hospital because the bite seemed pretty bad to me. Almost like it got infected right away, but he got all mad at me for saying that and told me he just wanted to go home and drink his killer headache off."

"Headache," Dave breathed. "Not good."

Amanda tilted her head, still not getting it. "So I did what he said. But when we pulled in the garage, he started acting weird. He grabbed for the wheel. I got nervous and I hit the gas when I meant to hit the brake. We swerved and smashed into the wall."

"Yeah, we saw your car downstairs," I whispered.

"He was still trying to grab me even after the accident,

so I ran away. Jack usually yells, he never hits. I thought if I just let him calm down, he'd be sorry later. But he followed me upstairs." She shivered. "I locked the door before he got in, though, and he didn't have his key. He pounded for a little while before he gave up. I haven't seen him since."

"Did you happen to have our house key in your car?" Dave asked with a sigh.

"Yeah," she said. "I guess we did. Why?"

I shook my head. "Before I get into that, can you tell me how long it took from the time Jack came out of the Gas Guzzler to the time he tried to attack you in the car?"

She shrugged. "About ten minutes."

Dave set the bat down. It was pretty clear that if Amanda hadn't turned yet, she probably wasn't going to. Lucky girl. I was kind of surprised, honestly. The week before I wouldn't have given Amanda five minutes in a hypothetical zombie attack.

"So what do you think happened to Jack?" Amanda asked, looking at her bandage job. To my surprise, it was still perfectly tied. It seemed our little Amanda had some talents after all. I never would have figured it.

"Okay, here's the thing, Amanda," I said as I took a deep breath. "When zombies bite a non-infected human, it changes them into a zombie."

"So?" Amanda paled as what I said started to sink in. "*Oh*...so you think the guy at the gas station who bit Jack was a zombie."

I nodded. "I have to assume so since even the hungriest homeless guy hardly ever bites someone. I guess there must be some amount of time between when someone becomes infected and when they lose all their humanity and ability to reason and higher brain function. During that time, I have to assume that Jack not only came up here and used our key to get in..."

She nodded. "He knew you had a key to our place. Maybe he was looking for that."

Dave drew back with a look of surprise. That hadn't actually occurred to either of us, but it made perfect and horrifying sense. If Jack wanted to get to Amanda and eat her brains, our place was the one way to get to her without breaking down the door, which he was apparently too lazy to do, even as a zombie.

"Good thought," I conceded and she grinned with pleasure. "Anyway, once he got here, he ended up roaming into our bathroom and getting himself trapped in our tub."

Amanda's brow wrinkled. "Huh?"

Dave looked at me. "That's a good piece of information to have. If they have a little brain function *after* they're starting to have a hunger for human flesh...well, that could be bad."

"*Really* bad," I agreed with a nod, but I needed to tell the rest of the story before I chickened out, so I refocused on Amanda. "Anyway, I came home and well..."

I trailed off as I motioned her to the bathroom. There was no easy way to do this so I guess it was better to do it quick, like pulling a bandage off a wound.

She followed me and I took a deep breath before I opened the door, then stepped out of the way so she could see the corpse of her former boyfriend.

She didn't say anything at first, just stared at him lying face down on the floor. His black blood was pooling all around him and his hands were clenched into claws. Not to mention his head was totally bashed in.

I shifted, thoroughly uncomfortable with what I'd done. Hallmark didn't exactly make a card for this situation (well, they do *now*, but not then), so I wasn't sure what to say to her so that she'd understand I hadn't done this out of spite.

"He-he attacked me," I finally explained. "He wanted to bite me just like he wanted to bite you and I had no choice but to kill him. But I'm really sorry, Mandy."

She nodded before she glanced at me. Her face was pale, but she was pretty calm considering. "It's okay, Sarah. I was going to break up with him anyway."

I blinked, staring as she turned her back on her dead boyfriend and walked away into the living room like she was walking away from a squirrel she'd hit on the road or something. Of all the reactions I would have thought she might have, this was the last one.

"O-*kay*," I said as I shut the door again.

Amanda sat on our couch for a long time before she looked up at Dave. "So do you *really* think all this stuff has to do with zombies?"

He nodded. "Jack tried to eat you, right?"

She shrugged. "I guess he did."

"And the *things* that attacked us today were after the same thing—flesh, brains, blood...*us* to eat." He shook his head. "I guess *zombie* is as good a term to use as any other."

Amanda sighed. "So what do you think we should do? That little emergency lady on the radio says to stay at home and wait it out."

"Well, we're not so sure about that," I said, but before

I could finish Dave grabbed me by the elbow and dragged me to the corner of the room.

"Sarah, do you really want to tell her about our plans?" he asked, his voice low so she wouldn't hear us argue.

"Why not?" I asked as I shrugged his hand away.

"Because I'm not really certain she'd make the best travel partner through a zombie-infested city," he hissed. "She gets confused by Scrabble."

I stared at him, overcome by disbelief. "Are you saying we just leave her here, like a little kid, to take care of herself? I mean, she doesn't even have a car anymore."

I looked at her. She was watching us, still all innocence and confusion. She smiled.

He followed my gaze and after a long pause he sighed. He wasn't stupid. He saw the same thing I did when he looked at her.

"Yeah, I guess that wouldn't be cool," he muttered reluctantly.

"No. Not cool at all." I glared at him before I moved back toward her. "Sorry about that, Amanda. Anyway, we were thinking it might be better to try to leave the city and get someplace less populated."

She nodded slowly. "I guess that makes sense. If there are less people it means there might be less...zombies. Or whatever they are. Maybe we could even find someone to help us."

"If you want, you can come with us," Dave said from behind me.

When I glanced at him over my shoulder, he didn't look pleased, but resigned. Still, I appreciated that he made the offer when I knew his feelings about it.

"It'll be dangerous," I added. "If we do this, we're

going to have to stop along the way and get guns and food and other things. And we may have to fight off the zombies. You may have to kill things that look like people."

"Well—" She looked toward the closed bathroom door. Blood was starting to seep into the beige carpet in front of it. "I guess it's better to stick together."

I smiled. "I agree."

"And you won't have to stop for guns," she added with a sunny smile. "Jack had some."

Dave moved forward, his eyes wide. "He did?"

Amanda nodded with great enthusiasm. "Yeah, he had a safe in the bedroom."

"Do you have the key?" I asked.

The idea of not having to make a gun run, at least right away, was a very happy one. The less we were forced to stop, the less likely it was that we'd get bitten. Plus, I felt safer with a shotgun than a frying pan as the weapon standing between me and undeath.

Amanda shook her head. "No, he kept it on him at all times and wouldn't let me have a copy. He said he didn't want to keep it close to the safe unless he was there to guard it. It's probably in his pocket."

Now *all* of us looked at the bathroom door. I have to say, I was *not* looking forward to digging around in Jack's gross jean pocket, which was now all gooey and disgusting thanks to Dr. Phil. And the toilet seat.

Still, we couldn't ask Amanda to go key diving. Even though she was somehow feeling okay about the fact that Jack was dead, *that* was probably going too far.

"I'll do it," Dave said with a heavy sigh.

"Are you sure?" I asked.

He shrugged as we all moved together toward the

bathroom door. "Yeah, you killed him. The least I can do is find the key."

He threw the door open and stared for a moment at this guy who he'd called friend for a couple of years. I felt bad for him.

The thing about the zombie outbreak is that you get really numb to all the death and blood and bodies. It happens faster than you'd probably like to think, too. You may not believe me, but I know what I'm talking about.

Still, there are moments, little moments, where you really *see* how bad things are. This was the first one of those moments for David. His face was twisted and sad as he stared at the body in our bathroom and I'm guessing he must have been remembering some of the good times he and Jack had shared over the years.

I was about to step forward and offer to do it instead when he crouched down on his haunches and dug his hand into Jack's pocket. After some digging and grunting he pulled out a few keys along with a now bloody, foil-wrapped condom that made all of us say, "Ewwww," at once.

"Which one?" he grunted as he dropped the condom and held the bloody keyring out for Amanda to inspect.

She squealed, but when he shoved the keys into her hands, she took them and looked.

"This one," she said as she held out the smallest of the bunch.

He took it back as she dug into her pocket and brought out a little disposable handi-wipe like you get at the doctor's office or even some rib joints. You know, the ones with the wrapper that you can never get open without help? Well, she was about to bite it to tear the package open. I snatched it just before her mouth closed over it.

"It's got blood all over it from your hands, Mandy," I snapped. "Don't take the risk of exposure to Jack's zombie cooties. Go cut it open in the kitchen or just wash your hands in there."

She stared at the blood-streaked package in my hand and then she nodded and disappeared into the other room. Dave stared after her with horror and annoyance in equal measure on his face.

"Is she serious?" he asked me as he turned on me with a shake of his head. "Did that just happen?"

I nodded sadly. "Yeah. It did. But hey, if Jack really does have weapons in that apartment then we might be set. We wouldn't have to stop at a sporting goods store, which means less chance of encountering someone infected."

"No, you're right." He looked at the bloody key and grimaced as he wiped it off on his shirt, trying to find some little corner that wasn't already soaked in...well, stuff. You know. Zombie stuff. "So what's our plan with this?"

"I think you and I should go over to the other apartment together," I said, looking over my shoulder toward the kitchen. I could hear Amanda running water in the other room. "We can carry more back with two of us."

"Maybe you should stay here," he said. "It could be dangerous."

I stared at him for a minute and then pointed toward my bloody shirt, slacks, and arms. "I've killed at least two people already. Really?"

"Okay, just saying." He shrugged.

"Amanda's not as messy with goop as we are. Maybe we could ask her to stay here and start the food," I suggested. I was a little embarrassed that I was starting to get really hungry, despite everything I'd done and seen that day. "That way she'll feel useful. I don't think she'd be much help in a fight."

"As long as she doesn't end up wrapping the pizza in bloody shirts to take it out of the oven or something," Dave muttered with a shrug.

I went into the kitchen and Amanda immediately agreed to take care of the pizza. And once I showed her the directions...then *read* her the directions and reminded her about not touching anything bloody, I felt comfortable leaving her alone.

When I came back into the living room David had his baseball bat in one hand and he held out a big metal flashlight my Dad had bought for us when we moved to the city. We'd never used it, but it was pretty heavy.

"Here, I found this," he grunted.

I took it and tested its weight in my hand, then swung it around a bit like a sword.

"That will do," I said with a quick, nervous smile for him.

"Ready?" he asked as he opened the door.

"As I'll ever be," I muttered as he turned the doorknob and we set out into the dimly lit hallway.

CHAPTER 6

You and your partner are on the same side.
It's the side of the living.

We'd been bugging the super of our building to get better hallway lights put in for two years, but no amount of arguing or pleading from the tenants swayed him. At some point in the "negotiation," he'd threatened to raise our rent to pay for the upgrade so everyone had shut up and just dealt with the buzzing, dim hallways.

Now I hated the fat ass even more because the flicking yellow glow made the entire scene in the hallway all the more surreal and creepy. Trust me, we didn't need that, it was bad enough as it was.

There was blood on the door across the way from ours and a little smear of sludge on the wall next to our apartment. I had to hope both were from Jack and not some unaccounted for zombie roaming around on our floor.

David looked around, checking all the way to the end of the hall before he motioned me out of the apartment. "Let's go slowly and keep an eye out."

"I hear that," I whispered.

I kept close to his heels, watching every damn door as we slipped down the few feet that separated our apartment door from Jack and Amanda's. That walk normally took less than a minute, but that night it felt like an hour because we had to move with such care.

When we got there both of us stared at the bloody handprint on the wooden surface that just about matched the size of Jack's hand. I could almost picture him standing there in his stained t-shirt, wishing he could get in and attack Amanda. I wonder how long he had stood there before his addled brain remembered the key we had in our place. And how long he'd been in our apartment before he stopped thinking at all.

Both of us shivered at the same time.

Dave shook off his reaction first and tried the door. It was open, which made him roll his eyes. Even in an emergency and with a boyfriend who had attacked her, Amanda hadn't thought to do something so simple as lock it.

Inside, he bolted the lock behind us and we looked around. The apartment was laid out the same as ours, so that would make it easier. Or at least, it *should* have.

Now okay, I'm no Martha Stewart so I normally don't judge, but Amanda and Jack obviously didn't care how they lived. Junk was piled everywhere. There were game systems, clothing, even empty pizza boxes strewn across the floor and furniture. It was like children lived here.

I shook my head as we gingerly stepped over the biggest piles and maneuvered around sharp furniture edges that were wedged too close together. Let's just say this was not an optimal setting to go into battle.

"There could be ten zombies in here and we'd never know it," I said under my breath.

"Well, let's not think about that, huh?" Dave whispered as he gave me a brief look over his shoulder, but I noticed he lifted his bat a little higher.

Somehow we managed to make it through the mess to Jack and Amanda's bedroom door where she'd said the safe was. Taking a deep breath, Dave turned the knob and pushed, but instead of swinging open easily, it stuck. We looked at each other and I raised my flashlight.

"Did she leave the hall door open, but lock the bedroom and just not bother to tell us?" I asked, incredulous that even Amanda was that stupid.

Dave put his shoulder into the door and shoved.

"No, it's not locked. There's something behind it," he grunted as he pushed to no avail. Panting, he straightened up and stared. "I think I'm going to have to get a running start and force it."

I stared at him. "But um…"

He glared. "What?"

"What if it's a body back there?"

"Do you want the guns or what?" he snapped as he kicked some stuff on the floor out of the way to clear himself a little path.

Apparently he didn't care about my answer, because before I gave one he got a couple steps running start and hit the door and put all the weight of his body into his shoulder. There was a creak and then the door gave way and opened about a foot and a half. Just enough for us to fit inside.

Dave staggered as the door gave and half fell into the room. Immediately I tried to climb in over him, you know, in an attempt to protect him in case there *were* zombies waiting for us. But did he appreciate it?

Yeah, no.

"Sarah, shit that's my kidney!" Dave yelped as I tripped over him.

"I'm just trying to help," I snapped as I got into the room around him.

"Then get off!" he barked, slapping at my legs as he got to his knees and we both looked around.

Lucky for us, since we were distracted by yet another fight, there were no zombies waiting for us, or even any dead people on the brink of waking up undead. I peered around the open door and found only another pile of clothing that had been blocking our entry.

"Remind me not to ask her to do any chores," I said as I helped Dave the rest of the way up.

He smiled and I guess our little argument was forgotten for now.

"I'll make sure you don't lose your mind and do something so stupid." He frowned as he flicked a sock off his pant leg that had stuck to him in the fall.

I grimaced as I hoped it was clean, not dirty, but then I saw what we'd been looking for and forgot about Amanda and Jack's pigsty.

"There's the safe," I said with the same reverence I would have used if I saw Joss Whedon or something.

Amanda hadn't been exaggerating. It was a *big* safe, tall enough to hold long-barreled weapons, not just handguns. As Dave put the key in the lock, I prayed Jack wasn't just using it to store porno and Ho-Hos.

I'm not kidding you. When the door swung open and David stepped aside so I could see our bounty, I think angels sang. Seriously, I thought I heard choirs, because in that huge metal box were about ten rifles and shotguns, lined up perfectly along the rack. Boxes of shells were stacked on the shelf above. They were surprisingly neat and organized, too, considering the room was such a fucking wreck.

Dave grinned at me. "Thank God for the second amendment."

I laughed as I reached in to take a few guns. "This may not be what the Founding Fathers intended, but good on them."

As I positioned weapons over my shoulder by the slings one by one, David set his baseball bat aside and loaded one of the rifles. As he slid the action in place and clicked the safety off, our eyes met. For some reason, now that he had a loaded gun in his hands, the reality of the situation really started to sink in.

We were in fucking Zombie Central. And we had to get out.

"This is messed up," I said softly, reaching out to pat his arm.

"Yes, it is, baby," he answered as he took some handguns and put them in his waistband.

I giggled a little at the sight of him with four of them sticking out of his pants. It was like a Western movie on steroids.

He looked down at where I was staring and rolled his eyes. Apparently he didn't find it as funny as I did.

"Okay huckster, let's just get back to the apartment before Amanda burns the place down and we have to run into the dark and zombie-infested streets."

I didn't answer, but since that was actually a distinct

possibility, I got moving toward the door. Before I could open it, Dave grabbed my wrist and pulled me back a little.

"Wait, wait," he whispered as he stepped in front of me and peeked through the peephole. Once again, I was annoyed to realize he was right.

"So?" I whispered when he remained staring there for what felt like a long time.

"Mr. Gonzales is out there," he said as he shot me a look from the corner of his eye.

"The super?" I asked, my eyes widening in surprise. I don't think I'd ever seen him up on the third floor. Hell, he was hard to find in his own office downstairs. "Do you think the old bastard is actually checking in on residents?"

Dave shook his head. "I doubt it. I can't picture him giving a damn about anyone but himself. Still, he's not stumbling around doing that herky jerky dance the zombies all seem to have down pat, so do you want to risk talking to him and see if he's human? Or at least as human as he's ever been."

I nodded without hesitation. Just the thought of other living people was a good one. Even if it was that asshole.

"He might be able to help us," I said. "Or even want to join up when we leave the city. If we're going to get out of here, we might need more bodies. Um...you know, live ones. I don't think dead ones are going to be a problem."

Dave clearly agreed with my assessment because without further discussion he opened the door and called out, "Mr. Gonzales?"

The super turned to face us and seemed surprised to see us coming out of Jack and Amanda's apartment. Of course we *were* carrying an arsenal of weapons, so I'm sure that didn't help in the "shocker" department.

"What are you doing there?" he asked, his light Spanish accent sharp as he moved toward us.

He looked just as mean and obnoxious as ever and I found myself relaxing, even relieved to see the fucker. He was one little flash of normal in a world of chaos.

"Just getting some supplies," Dave said as he shut the door behind us.

Mr. Gonzales glared as he looked from one of us to the other. "That isn't your apartment."

"No, but the tenant, Amanda, is in our apartment. She said it was okay for us to go get the guns," Dave explained.

I expected the super to say something about the weapons, but instead he shook his head.

"Amanda?" Gonzales asked. "The little dumb one that lives with the big dumb one here?"

I nodded. Awesome. I wondered how he described us when we weren't around.

"That's her, but Jack..."

I stopped as I thought of poor dead Jack on my bathroom floor, just another victim of Dr. Phil.

Mr. Gonzales seemed to understand my silence. "He isn't okay, eh?"

Dave must have sensed my discomfort with the topic because he changed it. "Hey, is anyone else left in the building? Maybe we survivors could all meet up and talk about some strategies to stay alive."

Mr. Gonzales tilted his head and for a moment he just

stared at Dave. I shifted the six guns I had, three on each shoulder and they were starting to get really heavy. Why couldn't he just say something so we could go back to our apartment and I could put these damned things down before my shoulders exploded?

"Mr. Gonzales?" Dave asked, his brow wrinkling. "You *have* been watching television, haven't you? You know that there has been an attack or something, right? People are getting sick and trying to...well, *eat* other people."

Mr. Gonzales smiled. "Of course, I know that. Now why don't you get little Amanda and come with me? We'll find the others. I'm sure we can find others."

I stared. There was something weird about how he was acting, not that Mr. Gonzales had ever been *normal*. He always stared at my tits when he talked to me. Today, though, he was staring at my head. Not my face. My head.

He tilted his chin and in the sickly yellow lights of the hallway I caught a reddish glint in his iris. Actually it was more orangey as the yellow and red met.

"Fuck, David!" I cried as the situation became clear. "He's a zombie. He's transitioning!"

Mr. Gonzales smiled and through his clenched teeth a thin version of the black zombie sludge seeped through. The guns on my back were heavy and I must have seemed like the easiest prey because the super lunged for me. I tried to dodge, but couldn't quite get out of the way with my load of firearms slowing me down.

He hit my shoulder and I slammed into the fire extinguisher box. The sharp metal edge jammed against my skin and I couldn't help but cry out in pain even as I continued struggling to get away.

Gonzales grabbed for my shirt and caught a handful of the stained white linen. It tore as I yanked against him, but that only made him grip harder, fisting the material as he pulled me back toward him. I smashed into his fat belly, pulled to his clammy chest. He was so close I could smell his breath and it smelled like cigarettes and death.

The transition was happening faster now. His skin was graying, his eyes fully red as his mouth snapped at me like some kind of rabid dog. I strained my neck to get away, to back up but I could only manage six or eight inches of space between my face and his.

There was a huge bang from behind me and suddenly the teeth and head were gone in an explosion of acrid gun powder and smoky blackness. Brains splattered on the wall, on our door; they seemed to fly everywhere. I felt the back spray of them on my face and made sure to keep my mouth shut as I turned my head in horror.

The smell of cordite and blood hung in the air as I turned toward my husband. David stood to my left, his smoking rifle still positioned on his shoulder. He was panting as he stared at the headless corpse of Mr. Gonzales. The dead super slumped over and ended up propped against the fire extinguisher box at a weird angle.

He still had my shirt in his hand and I tugged helplessly to get free, but his dead, clenched fingers wouldn't open. Finally I tore the fabric, leaving a fluttering remnant of white caught in his hand. Like a flag of surrender.

"Are you bitten?" David asked, his voice weird and faraway to my ringing ears.

I looked at Gonzales again and shivered. The blood at his empty, gaping neck hole was black, not red.

Suddenly Dave grabbed me and pulled me away from the sight. He spun me around and shook me hard.

"Damn it, Sarah, did you get bitten?"

My haze cleared as I looked down at my arm. Our super had made finger-shaped bruises on my skin, but I didn't see any broken flesh or black teeth marks to indicate my certain doom.

"N-No," I stammered. "I wasn't bitten."

Dave grabbed me and pulled me against his chest in the hardest hug he'd ever given me. His heart was beating pretty fast. So was mine. Even though we'd been attacked before, this was different. I had been weighted down, too off-balance to really fight or escape. Without Dave there to save me, I would have been undead for sure.

He let me go and looked around. "There are probably more of them in the building," he said.

I nodded as we walked away from what was left of Mr. Gonzales. "He was only just transitioning, so he would have been bitten ten or fifteen minutes ago, maybe."

David didn't respond, but opened our apartment door carefully. "Amanda?"

She popped out from our kitchen with a sunny smile of welcome. I stared. Once again, the former cheerleader looked terrific. In the time we'd been gone, she'd changed out of her bloody clothes into some of mine and washed herself up, I guessed in the kitchen sink since I couldn't imagine her climbing over Jack in the bathroom.

She'd even found an apron some hopeful relative had gotten me when we got married. It said, "Cooking for two" with a little arrow that pointed at her belly.

Why hadn't I thrown that thing away?

She was a regular fucking Donna Reed now.

"Oh lookie, you found his guns," she said with all the excitement of a kid.

Dave stared at her, I think as stunned by her absolute obliviousness as I was. "Yeah. Didn't you hear the shot in the hallway?"

"Hmmm?" Amanda said. "Oh, yeah. I heard a bang. I thought it was a really loud car backfire. Did you have to fire the gun?"

Dave was gritting his teeth and I could tell that he was on the edge of a meltdown of biblical proportions. Honestly, so was I, but I thought he might not be able to control it, so I stepped in between them and placed a hand on his chest gently.

"Hey," I said to him. "Why don't you take all these guns and put them in our bedroom so we can figure out the weapons and ammo situation after dinner. Then maybe we could roll Jack into the hall or out the window or something so that we can each shower. I know I don't want this disgusting shit on me anymore and I'm sure you feel the same way."

Dave kept his eyes trained on Amanda for another minute before he looked at me.

"Fine," he said, the word accentuated as he reached out to take some of the guns I had almost died for.

He left me with a shotgun and shells before he went into the bedroom. I loaded the gun carefully.

"Better check the pizza," Amanda said in a singsong voice.

She was still totally oblivious to the fact that she had just narrowly escaped getting killed, and this time not by a zombie.

I shook my head as I went to the phone. By now I was

sure my parents were freaked out by the news of the problems in Seattle. In fact, as I stared at our machine, I was kind of surprised that they hadn't called already.

When I picked up the phone, I realized why. Instead of a dial tone to greet me, there was only a repetitious beeping sound that indicated the line was dead. I stared at the receiver for probably a full minute before I replaced it and went for my cell.

My bloody purse was in its usual spot by the door, though I swear I don't remember putting it there. I snatched my cell out of the side pocket, wiped a smudge of blood off the screen with my mangled sleeve and powered it on (I always turned it off in Dr. Kelly's office). But when it lit up, there were no messages on it, either, and the "No Service" sign glowed on the screen.

I looked back and forth between both phones in my hand as a horrible realization hit me. Whether by government assistance or zombie, we no longer had a way to call for help.

And no way to let anyone know that we were alive.

CHAPTER 7

Never go to bed angry. Terrified is okay.

Amanda was asleep on the couch by the time I finished logging the non-perishable foods and putting them into a couple of big boxes to take with us the next day.

Since I don't cook very often, I'm sorry to say we didn't have much of use in our cupboards. There was some old soup, a few Power Bars, a really sad box of store brand chocolate cereal. Oh, and Pop Tarts. Wonderful Pop Tarts in a variety pack I'd found on sale a couple of weeks before.

I hoped that Amanda and Jack's apartment would give us a little more booty when we stopped there on our way out, but after seeing the sad state of it earlier in the day, I somehow doubted it. In fact, I was starting to think I wouldn't want anything they had.

Another box and a backpack sat by the door as I entered the main room. Those contained our weapons cache which now consisted of the guns, ammo, a big butcher cleaver I didn't even know we owned, Dave's baseball bat and my heavy flashlight. Once again, I wished we had more. Where did people find their missile launchers in zombie movies anyway?

Still, it would get us going and I hoped we'd find provisions along the road, or even make it to someplace untouched by the outbreak where we could just go to a store and resupply while we waited for all of this to blow over.

I walked to the couch and looked down at Amanda. She was a couple of years younger than me and right now she looked even more than that. Like a teenager and in some twisted way I'd become a twenty-seven-year-old Mom to her. My only consolation was that she was out of the diaper phase.

I grabbed a blanket from the back of the other chair and spread it over her. She didn't wake up, though she did snuggle down deeper into the couch cushions.

I shook my head as I moved away from her. I had no idea how she could do it. I doubted I'd be sleeping much tonight, that was for sure. Not with zombies still roaming around the apartment complex. But I guess she somehow trusted that Dave and I would take care of the situation...and her. Which was sweet in a really weird way.

I walked into our bedroom to find Dave already under the covers. The loaded rifle was propped up on his night-stand and I could see he had put some easily slipped on shoes at the ready, too. I did the same and put my shotgun within reach before I got in beside him.

The smaller television we kept on the dresser was on and he was watching some channel. This time it wasn't CNN since we don't get cable in the bedroom, but a local affiliate that had gone all news all the time in the crisis. You know, "Zombie Watch, 2010."

A really freaked-out anchorwoman with no makeup was sitting at the desk.

"Let me repeat that information again. Yes, the phone systems in the Greater Seattle area are currently down. And we've had reports that most cell phones are also not getting service. State and local governments have denied any involvement in the loss of telephone communications, and it may have to do with an outbreak of the plague at a local tower facility earlier in the day."

I moaned. "Maybe it's just crappy reception."

"Told you to upgrade to a better system," Dave said as he leaned forward and continued watching the small, fuzzy screen. "Can you hear me now?"

"Right now we can update you with some shocking numbers," the anchor continued. "The Centers for Disease Control is telling us that based on the aggressive spread of the outbreak, up to a million residents could already be stricken with what people on the streets are calling *zombieism*."

"Ha," Dave said in a flat tone and shot me a look. "Told you so. Did I call it or what?"

"I'm sure you thought of it first, dear," I said as I patted his arm.

"I'd like to go now to Dr. Emmett Elias, a University of Washington professor who worked in the lab where the outbreak apparently started. Joining us in the studio is Dr. Elias. Thank you for braving the drive across town, sir."

The camera panned back, and sitting next to the woman at the anchor desk was a fat, balding man in a really bad suit. Like beyond Men's Warehouse. I did *not* like the way he looked.

"Thanks for having me, Karen," he said with a smug smile.

She frowned at him. "Dr. Elias, can you tell us exactly what your lab was studying that could have caused such a terrible outcome as we've seen in our city today?"

The guy looked at her, his gaze sharp and his lips thin with anger. "No, I'm afraid I'm not authorized to discuss what we were specifically studying in the lab."

The reporter stared at him and Dave laughed. "She's ready to punch the guy, look how freaked out she is."

"I hope she does," I said as I glared at the doctor. "Asshole ruined my city and nearly got us all killed."

"Sources have told us that there may have been some government grants associated with the research," the reporter pressed. "Was this some kind of government program? What branch was it related to?"

The researcher's beady eyes narrowed. "Well, it *is* a state school, Miss Finch. Federal and state funding helps us provide many programs."

"And do most of those programs lead to everyday citizens turning to cannibals all around us?" the woman asked, her tone rising enough that it was clear she was as on edge as anybody. "Do you know that I saw a five-year-old child eating a *cop* on the way to the studio tonight, Dr. Elias?"

There was some hustle and bustle off-camera and the reporter blushed as she glanced at the screen. "I'm sorry. But you must see that people deserve to know more about what has caused this terrible outbreak that seems to be spreading at an outrageous rate."

Dr. Elias looked at her, tilting his head. I frowned. The way he was moving reminded me of something.

"It's quite all right, Miss Finch," he said. "You have lovely hair."

"He's a zombie," Dave whispered from beside me.

I nodded because the second the doctor complimented the reporter on her hair, I realized that his twitchy, weird movements reminded me of the super in the hallway. Mr. Gonzales had also turned his head all weird as he looked at me and so had Dr. Kelly before she attacked in her office. All zombies reminded me of a dog in an alley or the freaking alien in the *Alien* franchise.

I think the reporter realized what he was at the same moment because she let out a gut-curdling scream and pushed her rolling chair away from the desk. But she wasn't fast enough. The doctor lunged across the space between them and grabbed her. He yanked her close and then his teeth sank deep into her neck.

Dave and I both lurched back with combined cries of, "Oh!", like we were watching football or something. Red blood spurted around his black teeth from the wound, spraying across the desk. A few little specks even hit the camera lens so now we watched the rest of the horrifying scene through a slightly reddish haze of smeared blood.

A whole bunch of people came running from all directions. See, they still ran *toward* an attack in those days because we were all so shocked by what was happening around us. I guess we figured we could do something. We hadn't fully realized that wasn't any way to help someone who was bitten except to blow their head off before they turned into the living dead and lost all control of who and what they were.

A group of four men grabbed for the doctor, who was pulled off the bleeding, wailing reporter. She lifted her hand to her neck and when she saw blood coat her fingers, her screams grew even louder. The zombie doctor, both in that he created zombies and now was one himself, groaned and smashed his teeth at his captors. His higher brain function was clearly gone now and he thrashed about like a trapped animal.

Someone grabbed the boom mike from the stand above and starting hitting him until the doctor and the crew who held him slipped off frame behind the desk. The only thing we heard were growls and the only thing we saw for a minute or even more was the crewman's hand as it lifted up and then slammed down behind the desk. With each smashing blow the mike came up more bloodied and gruesome.

The reporter lay across the desk now, blood pooling under her head as she whimpered softly. But I already could tell she was starting to transition. Her posture went from weak to something more ready. And when she lifted her head, her eyes had a red glow that had nothing to do with the bloody camera viewfinder.

"Oh no," I whispered. "Those poor people."

Sure enough, she turned toward the group of men who had just tried to save her. With a crazy grin, she dove down amongst them with a guttural scream and then the screen went white with just the words, "We are experiencing technical difficulties. Please stand by."

Dave opted not to follow the neatly printed directions on the screen and instead clicked the TV off. We sat in silence for a long time, staring at the black screen. Finally, I rolled over on my side to face him.

"It's getting worse," I said after the silence had stretched out a long time.

"It seems to be," he agreed.

"If there are a million infected in less than twenty-four hours," I continued, "by the end of tomorrow half the city or more will be gone. So is the plan the same?"

He thought for a moment and then nodded slowly. "With the telephones out, the power is probably next, and I'd rather not be in the city when they shut her down completely. I think it's going to be mass hysteria."

"It's a crappy neighborhood anyway," I said. "Between the thugs and the zombies, we'd be fucked if we stayed."

He shrugged. "I say we get up early and get moving as soon as it's light out. My sister lives what...a hundred and thirty miles south in Longview? Maybe that will be far enough away. And without traffic to slow us down, we might even make it there in less than two hours."

I groaned as I flopped back on the pillows in dread and frustration. "Gina? You want to run to *Gina* in a crisis?"

There was a long pause as Dave clenched his teeth. Finally, he asked, "Why not?"

I looked up at him. "Um, she fucking hates me for one."

"I always figured the feeling was mutual," he said, his eyebrows lifting. "Come on, admit it, you never really tried with her."

I folded my arms. Okay, so I'll tell you something I never would have admitted to him. He was right (again, that asshole). I *hadn't* ever really tried with Gina.

She was only five years older than us, but acted like

a mother. A really boring, plaid-wearing mother. And she doted on David. Nothing he could do was wrong, which meant everything *I* did was. When we were with her, he acted like her little brother, not my husband. And he deferred to her, never taking my side if we disagreed.

I *hated* visiting her.

"Okay, how about this, which is worse," he asked. "Zombies or Gina?"

I hesitated too long, I guess, because he grabbed the pillow behind him and swatted me with it playfully. I laughed as I fended him off.

"Okay, okay, zombies are worse," I admitted. "But just barely."

He pushed the pillow behind his neck but remained lying on his side looking down at me. As I stared up at him, I realized we hadn't been so close in bed for a long time. I'd forgotten how nice it was. And he smelled good since we had tossed Jack out the window earlier in the evening and taken showers to clean up.

"Thanks," he said softly. He reached down and brushed a little damp hair off my cheek. "I know you hate going down there. I think I even get it, though I wish you liked my family. But I have to see if she's okay, at least."

I nodded. Okay, so I got that. I wondered about my family, too, but Gina was closest.

"This is going to be really dangerous, isn't it?" I asked, my voice soft in the dark.

He didn't answer for a long time, but finally he nodded slowly.

"We might die," I continued.

He nodded again, his gaze never leaving my face.

I reached up and cupped the back of his head and drew him down toward me.

"Well, I guess we better go out with a bang."

He smiled before he dropped his mouth to mine and kissed me.

CHAPTER 8

Give each other compliments every day.
Even when the undead attack, it's nice
to feel pretty. Or badass.

I should have known that having "end of the world" sex wouldn't solve our problems. Though, it was pretty great and I highly recommend it. It's one of the big benefits of an apocalypse that no one tells you about. It just makes everything...*better*, because you know it might be the last time every time.

But despite all that, by the time we were traveling down to the parking garage the next morning, David and I were snipping at each other again. It was like our mind-blowing night had never happened.

I guess it had all started up when I woke up in the middle of the night with a stunning realization. I hadn't checked the Internet! I had bolted from bed and logged on to our ancient desktop to find that I did have mail, as the old AOL saying used to go. One, from my Dad, dated earlier the previous day. His tense one-sentence, "Are you okay?" had said more than any page-long tome could have.

After shooting him an e-mail to let him know we were all right and planning to leave the city, I'd told Dave I wanted to go to San Diego and that had started a three in the morning bruiser about the intelligence of heading to another highly populated area.

I knew he was right that it wasn't smart and that we should stick to our original plan to go to Longview and see how things were after that, but I wanted my Daddy in that moment. So now this morning we were back to fighting.

"I'm just saying, maybe we should have checked a few more of the apartments in the building for supplies before we left. You never know what people have in their cupboards," I said as the elevator moved down floor after floor slowly.

Dave glared at me. "And risk bumping into a passel of zombies who could be hiding in any part of that building? No fucking way am I dying for some extra Power Bars! No, thank you. We've got enough supplies, at least for the time being. We're not going very far."

I looked at him incredulously. "Come *on*, David! It might take us longer than we think to get to your sister's. And she might not even be there when we get there. The last thing we should do is find ourselves stuck in some podunk town at the Washington/Oregon border without any supplies."

"As opposed to going to...say...*San Diego*?" Dave clenched his gun tighter, his eyes straight ahead. "Oh, big surprise, Sarah, you bagging on my family, my ideas, my—"

Amanda frowned as she adjusted the hand truck we'd found buried under at least five loads of laundry in her old apartment.

And why did she have a hand truck?

Well, it turned out it tired poor old Jack out to take the garbage out by hand, so he'd stolen a hand truck from the loading dock at his job. Annoying story, but it *was* helpful for transporting boxes of food, ammo, and the backpack stuffed with extra guns.

"Guys, as entertaining as this all is," she said, "the elevator is about to open and my hands are full, so I'll need you two to figure out if there are any zombies around. I don't really want to get killed because you two are fighting over...um, whatever it is you're fighting over."

I scowled at Dave as I cocked the shotgun. The sound of the slide of a shotgun is awesome. Dave popped the safety off his rifle just as the elevator slid open. Our twin glares said we'd finish this discussion later, but for now we concentrated on the task at hand.

Gingerly, we moved forward like some kind of trained unit of the military. Yeah, we catch on quickly. I looked to the right, scanning the garage for any sign of movement or infestation. Dave did the same on the left.

"Are we clear?" I asked as the three of us slipped from the elevator posed like some kind of ridiculous Charlie's Angels. Only Amanda really had the hair for it.

"Clear," he verified.

We inched forward. The garage was in far worse shape than it had been the night before. Amanda and Jack's wrecked car had been flipped onto its roof at some point. I guess the zombies must have wondered if there were easy victims inside waiting to be eaten.

Blood slashed one wall of the garage. A *lot* of blood. I shivered as I wondered if it was one of our former neighbors who had lost their battle there or just some poor soul who had managed to get inside thinking it might be safer. Wrong choice, for sure.

"It looks like lots of activity here last night," David said, motioning to the other side of the garage.

More pools of black sludge and blood sat beside a few of the cars that were haphazardly parked at odd angles.

"We'll have to be extra careful," I agreed. "Amanda, stay close and don't be afraid to drop the hand truck and run if it comes to that, okay?"

She nodded as we reached our car, but her pale face told me how terrified she was at the prospect of seeing a fully transitioned zombie since she hadn't yet had the pleasure.

When we reached our old beater, I peered into the backseat, but there was nothing lurking there.

"Car seems clear."

"I'll check the trunk," Dave said, positioning his key. When I looked at him incredulously, he said, "Hey, Jack got into our tub."

I shrugged one shoulder. "I guess that's true."

I stood guard beside Amanda. We both looked around nervously as Dave cleared the trunk. He motioned to her and she wheeled the cart to the back of the car. Together, they loaded the food into the trunk, leaving out only a few things for our trip down to Longview.

The guns and ammo we had decided to put in the backseat, so Amanda opened the back passenger door and began work positioning the weaponry for easy access.

"I still feel like it's not enough," I said as I looked at the car with worry.

David slammed the trunk hard enough that the car shook.

"Sarah, God damn it, nobody knows if we're doing this right or not. Seriously, maybe you're right! Is that what you want to hear?"

I opened my mouth, but apparently he wasn't done.

"Maybe we'll get ten miles up the road and be wishing we brought more fucking Pop Tarts. Or maybe we'll get all the way to Gina's without incident and find out that the rest of the universe is safe and happy. I have no fucking clue and I'm doing the best I can."

I stared at him. For all our snipping and all the strain in our relationship over the past six months, it was pretty rare for him to snap and say what he felt. Now I stared at him and I saw the strain on his face.

"You're right," I said through gritted teeth. "I'm sorry. We're both doing the best we can in a bad sit—"

Before I could finish the thought, a blood-curdling scream echoed from the backseat of our car. I spun toward Amanda and found her half in and half out of the vehicle, pointing wildly toward the garage gate that led to the street.

"Look!" she screamed over and over. "Look! Look! Look!"

Dave saw them first. "Fuck!"

Three zombies were coming toward us from across the garage. I recognized one as a homeless guy who stood near the bus stop every morning hawking the charity newspaper *Spare Change*. The other two I didn't know, but one of them was fucking huge. Using the car roof as a place to balance my weapon, I took aim as best I could and fired off a shot.

Okay, so I wasn't so good with a gun at the time, but with a shotgun you don't really have to be. The buckshot just flies out like a net and catches anything nearby.

I managed to hit the biggest zombie in the shoulder and blew off a chunk of his rotting flesh. He paused for a minute and looked down at the injury. His mouth twisted like he was mad, as well as totally confused, but then he started toward us again, this time at a much faster and more purposeful clip.

Next to me, Dave fired his gun and dropped the homeless guy in one hit. I reloaded my gun by opening and shutting the chamber at the same time he did and this time when I fired the zombies were close enough that I hit the big guy full in the face and chest and he whined as he fell backward and hit the concrete floor with a thunk.

The third zombie kept moving forward and surprised me by launching himself over the low roof of our car. He slid between Dave and me and snapped his mouth at me. I barely dodged as I staggered backward and hit the still open passenger door. Inside the car Amanda was cowering and screaming.

"Gun's jammed," Dave called out as he frantically tried to fix it.

I guess I should have fired my shotgun, but like I said I was pretty new to all this then. Instinct kicked in and instead of firing my perfectly good gun, I swung it. The butt met the zombie's face with all the force in my body and there was a satisfying wet thud.

The creature roared in pain as I shattered his nose and caved in part of his head. I ignored any pity I might have once felt for another living creature. I had to remember that this creature *wasn't*. He was nothing more than a crazy animal who needed to be put down.

With that in mind, I swung a second time and this time he didn't make any more noise because he was dead.

Well, I guess no longer *undead*. A vague, but important distinction.

Amanda was still screaming. Her thin, piercing wail traveled through the parking garage and bounced off the concrete walls so that it echoed back to us in an eerie, never-ending cry.

I stared at the dead body on top of my car. I stared at the other two on the garage floor. Then I stared at my husband. He was smiling at me. *Smiling* even though we had just bumped our formerly human, currently zombie killing spree up to a nice round six (not counting Mack, since we didn't actually know if we'd killed him when he flew off my car in the parking complex).

"Amanda, it's over. For the love of God, shut up!" I snapped with a roll of my eyes.

I moved out of the way so I could close the back passenger door of our car. Her cries continued, but they were much quieter behind the shut door and then they finally trailed off entirely. Through the smeared glass I could still see her lying in a fetal position on the backseat, twitching with fear every once in a while.

"What?" I asked, because Dave's smile had gotten wider. "Why are you looking at me that way?"

He shrugged as he moved around toward the driver's seat. Before he got in, he grabbed the car zombie's ankle and yanked him off the roof with a violent tug. I heard him hit the ground below with a wet and somehow also crunchy *smack*.

"Nothing," Dave said with a shrug as he stood at the driver's side door. "I was just thinking how much cooler you are than any other girl I ever knew."

He opened the car door and Amanda's low whimpers

greeted us. He motioned his head toward our guest. "Especially this one."

I couldn't hide my own smile as I got in the car. Putting on my sunglasses, I looked at him from the corner of my eye. "Okay, David. Let's roll."

CHAPTER 9

Make requests, not demands. "Please" kill
that zombie, honey, I'm out of bullets.

Dave didn't have to open the window to enter our garage
code because some time during the night the heavy,
metal gate had been torn from its hinges. Without further
incident, we pulled out onto the surface streets and Dave
began to dig around under his seat as he kept one hand
on the wheel.

"What are you doing?" I asked.

"Looking for the stereo button that broke off."

I couldn't help but chuckle. "That *you* broke off," I
corrected him.

"Is it this?" Amanda said from the backseat and
she held out the little button. "It must have rolled back
here."

I took it with a brief look toward Dave, but he was
staring straight ahead, his mouth a thin line of irritation.
I laughed as I fiddled with the button until it slipped back
into place and I was able to turn the radio on.

They weren't playing the "stay in your houses"

bulletins anymore, so we all sat quietly as the voice on the radio droned on about the plague spreading throughout and even beyond the city. Even if they hadn't talked about it, we could see the devastation for ourselves.

Up and down the streets, there were burning cars and broken windows. Buildings were slashed with blood and sidewalks pooled with it, but there were no bodies.

I guess because there were zombies, instead.

Hundreds, maybe thousands of zombies lurched along the blocks that led up to the highway. They dragged themselves along side streets, they carried mangled and broken limbs in their mouths like wolves with bones of prey. And they came in every shape and size, women and men, they were of every color, there were children and toothless grandparents.

"God," Amanda whimpered from the back.

"I'm not sure there is a God," I said softly. "How could there be in the middle of all of this?"

Dave didn't say anything. He just kept his eyes on the road, maneuvering around debris and powering through intersections where the zombies seemed to wait for potential victims. Eventually he managed to make it to the highway and we edged the car down the high-walled onramp.

When we reached the actual highway, all of us gasped. The day before when we had made our way to and from Dr. Kelly's office, the traffic had been so light that it was creepy. Obviously residents of Seattle's first response to the crisis had been to go home or stay at work, just as the bulletins had advised.

But as the local and national news coverage had gotten worse and worse, it seemed like the entire city had come to the same conclusion we had: that it was time to run. Only many of them hadn't waited until morning. They had ventured out into the dangerous night without a plan.

From the empty cars that were lined up, bumper to bumper in every lane to the bloody pavement beneath them, it was clear the freeway had become a deadly battlefield in the last eight or ten hours.

"Holy shit," Dave muttered beneath his breath. "Look at that."

I followed his gaze upward and sucked in a breath through my teeth. On the overpass was a hanging highway sign. You know the kind—the electronic ones that give out Amber alerts or warn about highway construction. Only this one now read, WARNING: ZOMBIES AHEAD.

"Whoa," I said as we rolled slowly underneath the sign. "Hey, I've read about those! It's a hack of the system. They've done them all over the world."

Ahead of us, a legless zombie dragged himself along the shoulder, holding a severed hand in his mouth that he worried like a dog with a bone, shaking it back and forth. Eventually the pinky finger broke off and flew out of my line of sight.

"I'm not sure it's a hack this time, Sarah," Dave said as he gripped the steering wheel tighter.

I didn't respond. Amanda only shivered in the back and for a while we rode in silence.

Dave maneuvered the car through the wreckage and for the first time in a long time I felt lucky that we could only afford this compact piece of shit. We were easily able to fit our way through small spaces that bigger cars would have struggled with.

"At some point we might have to move some cars," he finally said quietly as he looked at me out of the corner of his eye. "Can you handle it or do you want to drive?"

I swallowed hard. He meant I'd have to get out of the relative safety of our vehicle. Outside the possibility of a tangle with zombies was almost one hundred percent. But it had to be done.

I managed a nervous nod. "I-I can handle it. But..."

I turned around to look at Amanda. She stared back at me, wide-eyed and oblivious as usual.

"Hi," she said.

I smiled, hoping to keep her calm as I told her what I'd need her to do. "Hi. So Dave has to drive and I may have to move cars. But I need someone to cover me from the car with a gun while I'm out and can't protect myself as well. Do you understand what I mean?"

Dave's gaze flashed to me, "Sarah! She can't—"

"No," Amanda interrupted from behind us. "Look I know you think I'm dumb, David, and I guess I probably am. I just never had to do much after cheerleading. But I *can* learn things, you just have to explain them."

Dave kept driving in silence, his clenched jaw speaking what his lips wouldn't, but my smile for her grew wider as I motioned to one of the rifles on the seat next to her. You had to give the girl points for being willing to try.

"Okay, Amanda. Here's the thing about loading a gun..."

For the next ten minutes I explained the mechanics of the rifle to her and got her to the point where she seemed pretty comfortable with both loading it and clicking the safety on and off.

"Are you ready to try a few shots?" I asked as I used the power window button to roll down her window partway.

"We can't waste ammo, Sarah," Dave said and I could tell he was trying hard not to snap.

I glared at him. "Well, I'd rather not have her shoot *me* because she hasn't practiced. If you feel like that's wasting ammo, please let me know."

He let out a sigh that told me everything, but he nodded. "No, you're right. Just don't do too much. We might regret it later when there are zombies."

"If you see zombies, Amanda, shoot for them. Otherwise, pick a target and squeeze the trigger gently," I said, hoping to reassure her. She looked pretty nervous and Dave's attitude wasn't helping.

She nodded as she braced the gun on the window ledge. "I'm going to shoot the window out of that van over there."

I nodded at her choice of targets and waited as she squeezed off the shot. It was pretty close to the mark and zinged off the side mirror instead of the window. Amanda made a little noise of frustration and I reached back to pat her leg.

"It's okay, just try again."

Her second shot went better and the window shattered.

"I did it!" Amanda squealed, raising the gun up. It slapped the roof and she barely caught it as it slammed back down.

"Careful," Dave admonished her. When I glared at him, he smiled at her in the rearview mirror. "But good job."

She grinned before she popped off another couple of reasonably good shots.

"Okay, that's enough. Dave is right," I said. "We can't waste any more ammunition. But do you think you can stay calm and do exactly what you just did if there are zombies outside when I have to move a car?"

She looked nervous. Honestly, I *felt* nervous even as I tried to keep it together. She could easily shoot me while trying to "protect" me. I didn't relish the idea of having a hole in my shoulder while trying to fight off a zombie. For all I knew, the smell of my blood might even bring more.

"I can do it," Amanda finally said.

"Well, we're about to find out," Dave said as he motioned his head toward the road before us. There were six cars across, without any space to get around them on either shoulder.

I grabbed for a handgun from our stockpile in the backseat and made sure it was fully loaded before I popped it into my waistband. Slowly, I opened up the door and looked around for any zombies.

I hadn't fully gotten out when Dave grabbed my arm. "Be careful," he said softly.

I leaned forward and kissed him, hoping to reassure him even though there was no way to do it. The fact was that I was about to go into the fire and I might not make it through.

I shut the car door behind me, vaguely aware that Amanda was climbing up from the backseat into the front so she could pull off easier shots from my window.

My heart throbbed as I made my way up the highway. I pulled the gun from my back waistband and carried it at the ready as my eyes scanned from one side of the big highway to another. I tried to find a medium-sized car to move, hoping to create a large enough space that our smaller car wouldn't struggle to fit.

There was a red town car in the middle of the fray so I approached it with caution. It was too close to the big truck next to it and I had to wedge myself between the vehicles to look inside. As I peeked into the backseat there was a groaned growl that echoed from somewhere in front of me.

I leveled my gun toward the sound and pulled off a shot when a zombie dragged itself up along the shoulder. He fell instantly, dropping the bundle in his arms. When I saw it was a baby blanket, I made myself look away. I didn't want to see anything else, especially since whatever was in the bundle didn't cry.

Behind me another shot exploded and I looked over my shoulder to see that Amanda had dropped another zombie drooling black sludge into a car behind me. I raised my free hand to give her the thumbs up before I returned my attention to the town car. Its backseat was empty and it looked like a good prospect.

Immediately, I realized that I couldn't get the car door open with the vehicle so close to the one next to it so I used the butt of my hand gun to break the glass.

Carefully I dragged myself through the shattered window and turned the key that had been left in the ignition. As I put it in drive, I noticed a pool of blood in the seat beside me and shivered. The car inched forward until I bumped against another car.

I couldn't help it. I grinned as I slipped my seat belt into place.

Have you ever just wanted to smash a car? Or break a television? Or maybe burn a big fire in the middle of a city square? If the answer is yes, then you'd have some fun during a zombie infestation. It's the little moments, you know?

Anyway, I gunned the car and slammed forward, shoving the smaller vehicle in front of me. Throwing it in reverse, I backed up and slammed forward again, blowing the car in front of me out of the way.

I reached my hand out the window and motioned Dave forward. In the side window I saw him creeping our car through the space I'd made. As he pulled up next to me, I popped the glove compartment to see if the previous owner had anything of use.

Tic Tacs were all I got, but I pocketed them before I got out and started toward the backseat of our car. Hey, they were one and a half calories, right? In a pinch they'd provide *some* value.

Before I got back to our vehicle, a zombie opened the passenger door of a nearby SUV that had flipped on its side and half crawled, half fell out of the vehicle. This one was a woman dressed in what appeared to be some kind of stripper outfit. I stared, unable to help myself, at her skintight vinyl nurse's uniform that was unbuttoned to her bellybutton, which was pierced, of course.

But my shock at the ridiculousness of her appearance faded as she let out a roar and from behind her came five more stripper zombies, like she was their leader calling for a charge.

"Shit," I cried as I dove for the car. "Drive!"

I closed the door behind me and Dave burned rubber on the asphalt as the stripper zombies threw shoes at the vehicle and limped at us with that weird "Zombie Speed" that they seemed to sometimes have.

"Well," Dave said as we swerved around a broken-up motorcycle. "I'm guessing those girls may have been the day shift."

But none of us laughed even as I looked through the back window to see that we had lost them.

CHAPTER 10

Address one issue at a time. You can't load gasoline, pick up food, AND kill fifteen zombies all at once.

Well, we have a problem," Dave said after we had repeated the car-moving excitement a few times and made it all of five miles up the freeway.

I couldn't help but snort out laughter from the back seat. "Just *one*?"

"One more," he conceded with a glance toward me in the mirror. He looked nervous and my brow wrinkled in suspicion.

"What is it?"

He hesitated before he blurted out. "It looks like we're pretty low on gas."

I leaned forward and stared at the gauge over his shoulder. He was right, the needle was under a quarter of a tank. I glared at him. I knew he could feel it, even if he refused to look at me anymore.

I clenched my teeth.

"I thought you told me yesterday morning that you would fill it up before you picked me up at work to go to therapy," I said, trying really hard to keep my tone even but failing.

This was another of those bullshit things he did that drove me crazy.

"Yeah. I did," he admitted, his tone way softer than mine. "But I forgot."

"You *forgot*," I repeated as I flopped back in the seat and folded my arms. "*Great.*"

He was silent, but in the rearview mirror I could see his dark brown eyes boring into me. They were apologizing, but also sending me a message that he didn't need any additional punishment from me.

I sighed. "Look, I know you were busy yesterday," I finally said. "And how were we to know this would happen? I'm sure you would have stopped if you'd realized a zombie outbreak was on its way."

"I would have done a lot of things if I'd known that." He nodded. "But you only asked me to do one thing and I fucked up. Sorry."

"There's a Gas Guzzler right off exit 165," Amanda offered helpfully. "It's kind of busy most days, but I bet we can get in and out quickly."

Dave sighed. "Well, it's not that we think there will be a line, Mandy. It's more a *zombie* issue."

Her smile fell. "Oh. Right. I guess they *could* be roaming around there. A gas station *is* where Jack got bitten by that homeless guy."

I shut my eyes. She still didn't totally get this situation.

"Well, we're armed and we'll just have to be careful," I said, swallowing hard.

Dealing with the freeway zombies was scary enough. I

was trying not to think about surface streets where more of the horde would be roaming free.

Dave nodded as he worked his way to the exit ramp, got off and turned toward the Capital Hill area of the city. It was actually one of my favorite places in Seattle. There were a couple of universities up there and a lot of houses, stores and restaurants, plus the aforementioned Gas Guzzler which was right off the highway. We pulled up to a gas pump and Dave cut the engine.

It was quiet, but by this time we'd started recognizing the difference between quiet and *too* quiet.

"Okay, here's the plan," Dave whispered before any of us even unbuckled our seat belts. "I'll get out and start pumping the gas. You guys will have to cover me as best you can because I won't be able to watch my own back. Once we're done, we'll lock the car and go into the convenience store and get anything we can from the shelves."

Amanda nodded and so did I. With a brief look between the three of us, we each opened our door and stepped out with weapons drawn.

It's a weird thing to be in a city that is, essentially, dead.

Undead. Whatever.

I hadn't realized just how accustomed I'd become to the rush of cars on the freeway, the honk of horns, the chatter of people on the street, even the whine of airplanes up above.

Now there was an eerie silence that seemed as loud as any freight train. I shivered even in the warm summer air but forced myself to pay attention as Dave popped the gas tank door and moved around to start pumping fuel into our car.

I faced the front of the vehicle and Amanda took the back. Any movement was suspect, any sound made us lift our guns. But somehow, some way, we managed to keep from drawing attention from the infected the entire time Dave was gassing up. Finally he pulled the pump away and capped the tank.

He looked around. "I don't like this."

I nodded. "Maybe we should just go. Not try for supplies."

He stared at me. "Earlier all you wanted to do was search."

"That was then," I said. "This is now. Our task is to get to Longview and as slow as we're driving right now it could take the whole day to get past the airport, let alone to safety."

Dave moved toward me. "You're scared." I edged away, but he caught my shoulders. "We're *all* scared. But we're here now and we should look."

I looked toward the store. For some reason Dave was right, I was freaked the fuck out. More than I had allowed myself to be since this mess started. Maybe it was because the store was an unknown. A zombie standing three feet in front of me was starting to become commonplace. But I was scared about what I'd find in a convenience store.

"Come on," Amanda said with a bright smile. "Maybe we can find some antibiotic cream for the cut on my arm."

I sighed. I couldn't deny that request. We hadn't had many first aid supplies back at our apartment and certainly they hadn't either. It was only smart to keep all of us healthy as best we could and that meant preventing infection.

"Okay," I said quietly. I grabbed a handful of ammo

and stuck it in my pocket before I locked the car and followed Dave and Amanda.

The automatic doors were still working, which was a bad thing. There wasn't anyone in the store, which meant that whoever had been working at the time of the outbreak hadn't had the wherewithal to lock up the store.

We peered in as the door slid open. As it shut in our faces, I nodded. "Okay, it looks pretty clear."

When the door opened a second time, Dave stepped into the store with us behind him. It wasn't the biggest convenience store in existence. Probably three hundred square feet at the most, with six or seven low aisles of food. Coolers lined the back walls. Although the store had been unmanned for at least some amount of time, it hadn't been as cleaned out as I would have suspected.

In some way that made me nervous. No looting meant there weren't many humans left to loot.

Dave motioned toward the back of the store and I nodded, realizing he wanted us to clear the store from back to front. Amanda was less aware of pretty much *anything* around her, so instead of following us, she roamed away toward the aisle with cupcakes and candy.

Dave opened his mouth like he was going to call her back, but then he shut it and just moved forward. I angled myself to the other side of the room and did the same. I reached the back wall and looked for a moment at the cooler in front of me.

Beer.

Fuck that sounded good. Even though it was barely eight-thirty in the morning. But zombieism breeds alcoholism. It's true. Look it up.

I managed to get it together, though, and watching

David out of the corner of my eye, I moved along the length of the store, checking each corner and every cooler (hey, you never know, wouldn't it suck to reach in for a Coke and come out with a zombie gnawing your hand off?).

When we reached the front, we walked toward each other and met near the front door.

"It's so quiet. How can there be no zombies here?" I whispered.

He shook his head. "I don't know. But let's take it while we can get it."

He popped behind the counter and grabbed for plastic bags, which he handed out to us.

"Okay, ladies, let's shop," he said with false brightness. "Non-perishables, medical supplies, liquids if we can carry them are our priorities. If you're hungry right now, feel free to grab some perishables that you'll eat in the next few hours."

He stared at the walls of cigarettes and to my surprise he started pulling boxes off the walls.

"Um, are we taking up smoking?" I asked as I shoveled armfuls of beef jerky and chips into my bags. "I thought you were so against it, I mean the shit you gave me when I was trying to quit last year…"

He arched a brow. "They might be worth something to trade later."

I stared at him. "David, that's *prison* movies, not zombie movies."

He didn't answer, but came around the counter and dumped some candy bars into his cigarette bag.

"I have medical stuff," Amanda said, bring out a bag brimming with those materials. She'd picked pretty well as far as I could see. She had different sized Band-Aids, creams and even some painkillers. I'm not sure I would have stocked up so thoroughly from the selection in the gas station.

"All right then, let's go," Dave said, motioning us out the door.

"I'll drive if you want," I offered as the automatic door slid open.

"Yeah, that might...be...good..."

Dave trailed off and his bag hit the ground. So did mine. Even Amanda couldn't dumb her way out of this one. If the zombies hadn't been in the store, there was no shortage of them waiting outside. A group of maybe fifteen of them stood in a semi-circle in the area behind our car. And they were all staring directly at us.

CHAPTER 11

Share in your activities and interests.
If you're going to kill zombies anyway,
why not do it together?

In the group who greeted us, there were two zombie Starbucks attendants (probably from different Starbucks if I know Seattle), a zombie nurse (real this time, not a stripper), and at least one zombie fireman in full gear, along with a bunch of plainclothes zombies gathered around our car just... *staring* at us. Almost like they were waiting for us to say something.

For a minute we all stared back. I think we didn't really believe it was true.

I mean, we'd faced off with more than one zombie at a time before, but never this many and never in such an open, unprotected place. To make matters worse, most of our weapons were still locked in the car. We'd almost certainly have to get to them at some point if we wanted to survive the battle surely to come.

"C-Could we pretend we were zombies, too?" Amanda whispered in a tiny voice filled with fear. "D-Don't they sometimes do that in zombie movies?"

I gave Dave a side glance. "We could try it, right?"

"I guess so," he said slowly. Then he shook his head. "Yeah, I suppose it couldn't make things any worse."

I slid my bag of supplies up on my arm so that it hung out of my way and then I hunched the same shoulder lower, bending partly at my waist to give myself an off-balance appearance. I kept one hand at my handgun, though, hoping the horde wouldn't notice I was really at the ready.

Dave made a similar pose and we lurched forward as a team, making little moaning and whining sounds just like they did. Amanda followed us, her little fake zombie moans more like kitten mewls.

The zombies stared, their heads turning in that odd doglike way that was so off-putting. I think we confused them.

Okay, I *know* we confused them. I mean, they looked at each other with a few grunts like they were saying, "'What do you think, Zombie Bob?' 'Well, I don't know, Zombie Pete, let's see what they do next.'"

But it seemed like, against all odds, our ruse was working. I mean, I almost thought we had it made. We were *almost* to the car, *almost* to a reasonable level of safety, or at least to a way to blast through a few of the zombies who were in the way of our freedom.

And then Dave dropped his keys.

I think he must have been trying to fish them out of his pocket in a herky jerky zombie way and they slipped from his fingers. However it happened, they hit the ground with a jangle and he bent down out of habit to grab them. But the smoothness of his movements, or maybe the fact that he was trying to get his keys out like a human would, put the kibosh on any deception the zombies might have believed.

With a roar, four of them rushed forward at once. The rest followed at a slower pace, swinging their arms and gnashing their teeth.

"Guns!" I screamed, leveling my handgun and squeezing the trigger carefully.

My aim must have been getting better because one of the lead zombies crumpled as his forehead exploded like Fourth of July fireworks over Lake Washington.

Dave fired his rifle in rapid succession and another two zombies fell to the side, but now they were closing even faster. There was no way we were going to be able to drop them all from a distance, especially since Amanda was still standing behind us, staring at the approaching horde with a blank, terrified look on her pretty face.

"Amanda, God damn it, FIRE!" I screamed at her as I reloaded my gun with shaking hands.

But it was too late for that because the zombies had reached us.

The nurse zombie went for me and I flipped my gun around as her clawlike hands swiped toward me. Swinging, I hit her in the temple with the butt.

She moaned and whined as the rotten skin on her temple split, but her teeth still snapped at me even as I pushed her away.

My arms were starting to get really tired from all this hand-to-hand combat I'd been indulging in lately, so I shook as I tried to put enough distance between us to either smack her in the head again or fire off a shot.

"No," I whispered as the struggle began to overwhelm

me. Oh shit. This was it. I was about to die, er, *undie* and it really sucked.

But then, just as I felt the zombie's breath on my neck, Amanda ran up and swung the butt of her shotgun. It connected with the nurse zombie's skull and the light went out of her eyes as the side of her head caved in like a soda can being smashed by a sledgehammer.

I panted as I pushed the body off me. "Thanks," I said before I flipped the gun around and put a shot into the skull of another approaching zombie.

Amanda jumped in the opposite direction, hurling out a guttural war cry as she sprayed shotgun fire into the zombie crowd.

"Die, fuckers!"

I couldn't help but laugh at the phrase coming from Amanda's cheerleader/pretty girl voice that was far better suited to say, "Go team!"

As I fired again, I grabbed for the extra bullets I'd put in my pocket before we went inside. My hands shook as I slid one bullet after another into the cylinder. When I closed it up, I pinched that piece of webbed skin between my thumb and forefinger.

As I swore, I kicked a zombie in the chest like I'd once seen somebody do during an MMA fight David had made me watch. The zombie wore a trucker hat and a flannel shirt and was a big guy, so I assumed he had been a trucker. Or a whacked-out Ashton Kutcher/grunge fan.

Whatever, once I'd put some space between us, I shot him between the eyes. Right in the middle of the "Really?" logo on his dopey hat. Black sludge seeped out of the hole I left and stained the white fabric as he hit the ground face first with a crashing thud.

"Yeah, asshole," I said. *"Really."*

"Sarah!"

I spun to see that Dave had made it to the car and managed to get it unlocked.

I ran toward him, firing my handgun at a couple of zombies who had begun to turn in his direction like a weird herd of cattle. Rabid, flesh-eating cattle...

"I'm here, I'm covering you," I said as I put my back to his and continued to take aim at the zombies who were coming for him as he worked on weapons.

Even as I shot, I found Amanda. Although she'd started off the day screaming like a banshee over three zombies, now she seemed to have hit a rhythm in her killing method.

She blasted her shotgun through zombie heads, taking them off at the neck when they dared to get too close to her. She'd even gotten good at swinging her gun to get herself some space when she needed to reload.

"I'm out of shells," she called as she popped the last two into the barrel.

"I've got you, girl," I promised as I put a bullet in the last zombie who was lurching toward her.

She ran down to the car, smacking a stray zombie in the throat and sending it careening backward across the parking lot. I fired off a shot as it staggered back to its feet and it fell where it stood.

Dave handed off a box of shotgun shells to Amanda and a handful of bullets to me and popped out of the car with a handgun in his belt and a reloaded rifle at the ready, but as we looked around the parking lot, we realized there were no more zombies left to battle.

"Holy shit," I said as I looked from one of them to the other. "Did we just win?"

Dave laughed. "I think so. Nobody got bitten, right? Everyone is okay?"

We each looked down at ourselves and each other, but aside from some blood and a bit of gore splattered on us from the dead, everyone was actually okay.

"Good, we must be getting better at this," he said with a relieved sigh.

I nodded. "We could make it a career."

He chuckled as he took the bags of extra supplies we'd gotten into this predicament to obtain and tossed them in the backseat. "Yeah, I can see it now. Zombiebusters! Let's get the hell out of here."

"Wait," Amanda said. "I have to pee now."

Dave's eyebrows went up. "What?"

"I really have to pee." Amanda said as she squirmed. "We cleared the store, right?"

Dave was counting up the supplies and he rolled his eyes. "Yeah, yeah. Just hurry. We don't want another horde getting to us while we wait."

She was already running toward the sliding doors, her shotgun over her shoulder. "I'll be really fast! Don't leave without me."

I frowned at her last statement. Once she was gone, I turned back to him.

"You should be nicer to her," I whispered.

He looked up from the bags in the backseat with a glare. "C'mon Sarah. Whatever."

I stared at him. I didn't like this David who seemed to have no empathy. But maybe he just didn't get where Amanda was coming from.

"No, really," I insisted, searching for a way to explain. "I think she knows you didn't want her with us in the first place. She's trying really hard. And she *did* get to killing when we needed her."

"I guess," he grunted. "But I still worry she'll slow us down at some point."

I stared at him. How could he so coldly dismiss someone who had basically helped keep him…and me…alive?

"And what about me?" I asked. "Would you ditch me too if you had a chance?"

He didn't look up from his cataloguing of our new supplies. "That's totally different and you know it."

"No, I don't. What I *do* know is that you looked for a divorce lawyer online," I said.

He froze in his spot for a few seconds, then slowly set the bags of food and other supplies onto the floor on the driver's side of the car.

"And how do you know that, Sarah?" he asked without turning around.

I shrugged. "Because I did, too. I found it in your search history."

He stood up from the backseat and faced me. His face was like a mask, it was so still and emotionless. I don't know if he was trying to think of something to say, I guess I hoped he was, but he didn't get the chance. Before we could get into it, Amanda ran back to the car.

"I'm ready."

"Me too," Dave said, shoving around us to open the front passenger side of the car.

Because I was upset, I stopped looking at him and instead glanced at Amanda. She was disheveled, her hair messed up and her hoodie was torn.

"Hey, didn't you have less blood on you before you went in?" I asked.

She nodded, though her cheeks paled a little. "Yeah, um, there was a zombie girl in the bathroom. A little girl. I had to fight her."

I sucked in a breath at the idea. "Oh my God, are you okay?"

Dave hopped out of the car and stared at her. "Jesus, we didn't check the bathroom. Stupid!! Did you get bitten, are you hurt?"

When I think about it now, I remember that she hesitated. But at the time I was so freaked out by the fact that we'd just fought off a full zombie horde and then Dave and I said the "d" word we'd been avoiding for months. . . . I guess I didn't recognize it.

"I'm not hurt," she said as she smiled brightly and got into the car. "Let's just go."

"Are you sure?" I asked.

She shut the door but I saw her nodding through the blood-smeared glass. Dave didn't look at me, but got in, too. So I shrugged and went around to the driver's side and we headed back down the hill toward the highway.

CHAPTER 12

Build mutual friendships. Just be ready to end them when your friends start trying to eat you.

I lied."

I glanced away from the road to look at Amanda in the rearview mirror and Dave lifted his head from the glove compartment, which he had been searching through in hopes he could find something of use. Yeah, it probably sounds weird, but ask yourself, how often do *you* go through your glove box? There could be all kinds of useful shit in there and you'd never know it.

Of course all he'd found so far were four expired insurance cards and a pack of gum that was just this side of petrified. Still I respected him for making the effort. I certainly hadn't thought of it, myself.

"What? What did you lie about?" I asked as I slowed the vehicle to move it around another mass of cars. Several of them were on fire, broken husks of the life their probably undead owners once lived.

Amanda blinked like she was holding back tears and then she slowly began to roll up the sleeve of her hoodie.

I couldn't see what she was doing in the mirror, but I heard Dave suck in a hard, harsh breath as he looked back at her.

"Oh fuck, Amanda," he said. "Oh shit, fuck."

I glanced over my shoulder and saw what the fuss was about. Amanda had a huge bite mark on her arm where her sweatshirt was torn. Already, it oozed the telltale black sludge of a future zombie.

"Amanda!" I cried in horror.

I looked back toward the road and my horror turned to terror. There, sticking halfway into my lane, was a flipped semi. I swerved the wheel sharply to the left and just barely avoided a potentially fatal sideswipe, but I over-corrected just like they always tell you not to in Driver's Ed. We careened toward the guardrail with David bracing on the dashboard and Amanda just letting her body swish around limply, like she didn't care. And I guess at that point, why should she? Her fate was sealed one way or another.

With my heart pounding, I gripped the wheel and somehow managed to steady it before we slammed into the metal and concrete of the divider. The tires screeched in protest and the car tilted painfully, but we didn't crash.

Once I had the vehicle back under control, I glanced back at Amanda. How was this possible?

"I'll pull over," I gasped, hardly able to catch my breath as the reality of this situation sank in more and more. "I have to pull over so we can look."

"No!" Dave cried, motioning around us wildly. "Look, there are about a hundred of those things standing by the side of the road. You have to drive, Sarah. We can't stop right now or we'll *all* get bitten and that won't help Amanda."

My breath came out as a sob as I saw the zombies. He was right. They were standing by the side of the road, flinching and writhing as they watched our car roll by.

They were hunters now, the only thing left in their infected minds was the desire to eat flesh, suck marrow from bones, and draw whatever nutrients they got from brains. If we stopped, they'd charge and there would be no keeping them out of the car. We'd run out of ammo before we'd gotten rid of half of them, especially without Amanda to help us fend them off the way she had in the parking lot.

"Why didn't you tell us?" Dave asked, his voice loud, but strangely not angry. "Why didn't you show us this back at the gas station?"

I could see tears leaking from Amanda's eyes in the rearview mirror. To my horror, they were grey, not clear, and *not* because of runny mascara or anything.

"She was so little," Amanda said as she tightened her grip on her injured arm. "No more than five or six, probably. She had blond hair and an American Girls doll that's just like the one my niece has."

She sobbed for a moment, but neither of us interrupted.

Finally she continued, "She was standing in a stall all by herself and I swear I didn't know she was a zombie until she was on top of me. I just thought I could help her and then she was on me, growling and squirming and she-she bit me."

"Oh no," Dave breathed. "Oh, Amanda..."

"I-I thought you would leave me," Amanda sobbed. "I didn't want you to leave me so I lied when you asked if I was okay and I hoped I would be somehow. B-But now I can feel myself changing."

"Feel it?" David asked softly.

She nodded. "I want to bite you."

"Which *you*?" I asked as I swerved around a group of three zombies. Their fists pounded against the sides of the car as we passed them.

"Either one," Amanda sobbed. "It doesn't matter to me, really. I can smell your blood and your brains. I can *smell* them."

Dave stared at her. "I don't know what to do. What do we do?"

She swallowed, but it was clear that even that simple act was difficult.

"In the zombie movies, there's always a friend who gets turned. A-and they always have to kill them."

Dave shook his head. "*No!* No, Amanda. We can't kill you."

"You have to," she cried. Her voice garbled slightly and she had to suck in a breath before she continued, "In a minute I won't be able to stop myself from jumping forward to attack you. I'll go for Sarah first since she's driving and she can't defend herself. I'll dig my teeth into her neck and suck on her skin. I'll bite her until I taste her frontal lobe."

"Amanda," I said, unable to keep the shock from my voice.

As she turned into a monster, she actually sounded so much calmer, almost more intelligent. But I guess it made sense. As her brain shut down, what was left was stronger, if only for a moment. Kind of like a person who lost their sight and could hear better.

Only soon Amanda would be gone. She wouldn't retain any intelligence or humanity. She would be a thing. An ugly, horrible thing that didn't remember we were friends.

"David," she screamed. "Shoot me. Please kill me! Kill me now before I hurt you!"

He lifted the handgun that was on the center console between us. His hand shook as he leveled it on her, aiming for her head.

"Dave, no!" I cried, even though I knew as well as he did that this was the only way. Still, it was a sickening thought. Even after everything we'd already done, this was so different. "God, please...please! It's Amanda!"

"Do it," she moaned, but her eyes were starting to turn red. I saw the glitter of the iris in the rearview and my heart felt like it was exploding in my ears.

"Do—*arggh*,"

And she was gone. Amanda was gone. With a growl, she vomited black sludge across her pink tank top and she tilted her head at us. Then she smiled, her teeth greyed from the sludge and her tongue black.

"Kill it!" I screamed.

My attention was so split that this time I didn't notice the car that was turned on its warped and twisted side ahead of me. I wrenched the wheel like I had with the semi, but I slammed against it anyway, flinching as metal ground on metal. Dave's door split like a rotten banana as a long piece of the other car's bumper tore through the metal panel. Dave yelped and scooted toward the middle of the seat to keep from being sliced by the shards.

"Sarah, fuck!"

I swung the wheel away from the wreckage and the

passenger door tore off entirely, but we managed to break away and slide to the shoulder. But the road was just as bad there, where we bounced over glass and metal pieces from earlier accidents and explosions.

In the backseat, Amanda slammed to the side as the car careened and she let out an angry, hissing cry before she grabbed the back of both our seats and yanked herself closer.

"Oh God!" I screamed as I thought of what she'd said earlier about tearing my flesh with her teeth. "Shoot it! Please, shoot—"

Before I could finish the sentence, Dave fired the gun. At such short range, Amanda flew backward from the pressure of the blast. Blood, sludge and brains blew against the back window, blocking any view I had. Amanda, or what was left of her, slumped forward onto the floor of the backseat. She twitched once and then lay still.

"Fuck!" I cried as the car rocked, only this time it wasn't from my shitty driving.

Now that Dave's door was gone, the zombies along the side of the road seemed to sense our renewed weakness. Racing forward in small groups, they growled, swiping at Dave. He scootched closer to the middle console and cocked the gun he'd just used to kill our friend, firing into the crowd of them even while he reached into the backseat with his free hand to grab for a shotgun.

"Watch the road, baby!" he said. "You watch the road and I'll take care of this. Just please don't stop, whatever else you do."

I concentrated on the pavement ahead of me as best I could, swerving around cars, sideswiping zombies into the highway barriers when I was able to catch them.

"What do I do?" I yelled as I looked ahead of me at the long rows of cars still broken down and abandoned ahead. "It's so blocked up, I can't go any faster."

"Get off!" he barked as he tossed the empty handgun into the back and started firing off shotgun shots that made my ears ring in the close quarters.

I slung the car across several lanes toward the next off ramp, smashing broken vehicles as I went and rolling over flailing zombies as our car threw them to the ground. I gunned the sputtering vehicle up the exit ramp and hit the flipped motorcycle that was lying in the middle of the road. For a minute we went airborne and then hit the street with a crunching sound. It may sound cool or look cool when that happens in a movie, but in reality...not so much, especially since the engine started smoking the second we hit.

At the end of the exit, the way left was blocked by another overturned semi, so I roared to the right and headed into the heart of Seattle's International District, with zombies running up the ramp after us and our car lurching and coughing from all the hits it had taken.

The surface streets were actually less congested than the highway and it was easier to move around the cars and debris scattered along our route. As I swung the wheel from side to side in an effort to compensate for the damage done to the steering, I tried to look behind us, but my view was blocked by the splattered remains of Amanda's head. I forced myself not to puke.

"Can you see any of them?" I finally asked when I could breathe enough to talk.

Dave leaned out the gaping open side of the car and looked back toward the ramp we'd just driven up. "No.

They can't seem to make it off the highway, the exit is too steep for them to figure out."

I let out a sigh of relief at that. With the ones behind us stuck, there weren't any zombies, at least not where we could see them. I'm sure they were lurking around, but they hadn't figured out that Dave and Sarah's All You Can Eat Buffet On Broken Wheels was rolling their way yet. So for a minute, at least, we were safe.

"Look for a car dealership," Dave said softly as he reloaded his shotgun and reached in the back for the empty handgun and a box of bullets.

I kept my eyes straight ahead and didn't answer as I scanned around us and down side streets.

The International District was a funky place, with all kinds of ethnicities represented in the brightly colored shops and restaurants, though the culture with the biggest influence was Vietnamese. We had pulled into the area known as Little Saigon.

"There," Dave said, motioning down a side street I'd just passed. I came to a lurching stop, put the car in reverse (which elicited a great deal of loud protest from the transmission) and rolled the car back to turn down the narrow side street.

Dave was right. Sheesh, I end up saying that a lot. But there was no denying that up ahead was a gaudy car lot. "Happy New and Used Cars, We Work With Any Credit!" it touted with a garish sign that swung from the paws of an enormous inflated gorilla.

"Why do these joints always try to sell cars with inflatables?" Dave muttered under his breath. "So cheesy."

"We should try to get something new," I said as I came to a stop and put our choking, hissing car into park.

He nodded as he handed me a fully loaded shotgun along with a bunch of shells and got out. We walked onto the deserted lot and looked around.

"All the keys will probably be in a lockbox inside," Dave said. "Come on."

"We should get something big," I said. "Something that can move smaller vehicles because—"

I broke off. I didn't want to say why. Dave seemed to understand though. I mean, it was pretty obvious that without a third person in our party, moving cars out of the way was going to be way more dangerous. We wouldn't want to do it if we could use a big vehicle to push them instead.

We opened the big glass door that led to the showroom floor. Canned music was playing, "Highway to Hell" in muzak version and I shook my head as I looked at the convertibles that were showcased for the discriminating buyer. In Seattle. Where it rains practically every day. Awesome.

Dave motioned to a big desk in the back corner. A tall lockbox was attached to the wall behind it and that was probably filled with car keys for test drives.

I followed him, gun at the ready as he edged up to the desk. It was really tall and you couldn't see under it, so we shouldn't have been surprised when a female zombie jumped up from behind it and gave a roar of welcome.

She was dressed in a light blue polo shirt with "Happy New and Used Cars" blazoned across it in bright orange lettering. Oh yeah, and it was also splattered with black zombie sludge and little flecks of freshly eaten brains.

Inviting. I could tell my car-stealing experience was going to be "happy," indeed.

Dave fired off the shot that dropped her without even flinching and came around behind the desk to check that the job was done. He fired a second one out of my line of sight, I guess to be safe rather than sorry (a very good thing during a zombie apocalypse) and then bent over the corpse.

"What are you doing?" I asked as I kept an eye out for zombie stragglers.

"Getting the box key," he explained as he came up with a bloody key ring. "We might as well not have to waste ammo or time trying to force it. Keep an eye out."

I did as I was told while he fiddled with a few keys, testing them in the little round lock that held the box closed. Finally, the metal door swung open to reveal row after row of keys all arranged neatly.

Dave started calling out makes and models of vehicles for my approval, everything from completely crappy shitters like our now-dead car to really nice vehicles.

I had an opinion about which one to pick, I really did, but I didn't answer because from down a hallway toward the back of the office came two zombies. They were dressed in cheap polyester pants and ugly ties and both wore nametags, so I assumed they were sales zombies.

"Shit, I wouldn't have bought anything from these idiots anyway," I muttered as I fired off a shot.

One of the sales zombies flew backward as his head exploded like a watermelon. But the other leapt toward me before I could manage a second shot.

I backed up out of instinct and found myself falling backward over a low ottoman that had been placed near the sales desk, no doubt for customers to be comfortable during the wait for their terrible credit scores to be run by the fine sales crew.

I hit the ground and my shotgun skidded across the parquet floor out of my reach. The zombie was bearing down on me now and Dave swore as he grabbed for the handgun he had set down while he jimmied the lock.

I raised my hands in the hopes I could somehow hold the approaching beast off. The whole world seemed to slow to half time. He lunged over me, a ridiculous-looking zombie with a fucking goatee and an earring stuck through his gray, dead ear. Oh yeah, he also had a mullet. I was going to get killed and turned into a zombie by a guy with a mullet.

And then the strangest thing happened. Instead of dropping down and sinking his teeth into my flesh, there was a bang and the zombie let out a cry as a gaping hole appeared in his forehead. He collapsed down on top of me, but not in an attempt to kill me. The light went out of his eyes and he whined out a final breath as he died.

David raced around the sales desk and grabbed the zombie's mullet to pull his now-lifeless corpse off of me. As I got up, we both turned toward the door. Standing there, dressed like a character from Underworld or something, was a petite Asian girl carrying a huge shotgun.

"Hey," she said as she reloaded with one hand. "What's up?"

CHAPTER 13

Present a united front. You against the zombies.

I think we all must have just stared at each other for at least a full minute. Dave and I were honestly pretty shocked to see another human person. If you think about it, this was the first live human we'd found since the previous afternoon when Amanda came to our door looking for Jack. I wasn't even sure what to say to a stranger anymore.

As for the girl, well, she looked pretty unimpressed and bored by the sight of us. So I guess she didn't *have* anything to say.

"Um, thanks for your help," I finally said as I moved a little closer.

"No problem." She shrugged like saving my life was no thing. "I saw you guys pull in the lot from the apartment above the restaurant across the way. From the looks of your car, I figured you might need help."

Dave and I exchanged a look at her pointed statement, but then he smiled.

"Well, we did. And we really appreciate what you did for us," Dave said as he moved toward her with his hand extended. He'd always been good with people, that was why we'd thought he'd be so successful in business. "I'm David and this is my wife Sarah."

She didn't make any move to shake his hand. I noticed at that point that she was wearing plastic gloves. Also a mask like the ones painters wear dangled around her neck and as we moved closer, she lifted it up to cover her nose and mouth. It reminded me of all those outbreaks of things like swine flu when people had worn those masks to protect themselves in airports or stores.

But a mask wasn't going to do shit in this case.

"I'm Lisa," she said, her voice a little muffled by the white cotton that now covered her mouth. There was a long pause and then she motioned us toward the door. "My grandfather owned the restaurant over there. Do you want to come up and I'll share some of my food? It's perishable so it has to be eaten before we lose power."

I looked at Dave and he nodded. "It *has* been a while since breakfast."

That seemed to be enough for her, because she turned and glanced around the parking lot before she headed toward the back of a restaurant that faced the car lot. We followed her, keeping our eyes peeled for zombies, but the lot was just as quiet as it had been when we approached it.

Lisa took us through the back door of the restaurant, still fragrant with the previous day's food. My stomach growled and once again I was ashamed that I could want to eat after everything that had happened. But not ashamed enough to stop following her up the small hall that led to the main dining room.

The room was still pretty tidy with small tables arranged in a pleasing way around the room. Different sauces and salt and pepper still stood on their tops. There really wasn't a stick of furniture out of place.

From the looks of the place, one might have thought it was just a slow day...well, except for the bodies stacked by the front door and the fine spray of sticky blood slashed across the menu display above the counter.

I flinched as I counted the bodies swiftly. Eight. All of them headless. I guess Lisa, or whoever had killed them, hadn't wanted to take any chances with zombification. Smart. We'd adopt the same policy in time.

"This way," Lisa said as she opened up a door behind the counter with a key and took us up a flight of stairs to another locked door. She let us in and as we got inside the foyer of a tiny apartment she bolted the door and moved a big chair in front of it.

I looked around. The place was in an older building and it had that faintly musty smell of it, along with the strong scents of a thousand meals made below. But it wasn't unpleasant, just nostalgic and almost comforting.

"The food is in the fridge," Lisa said as she went into another room.

We followed and soon found ourselves seated at a chipped Formica kitchen table covered in traditional Vietnamese noodle soups and dumpling dishes. I took my first bite and moaned with delight.

Lisa looked at me sharply, I guess looking for signs that I was infected, but then I thought I saw her smile behind her mask.

"My grandfather was a good cook," she said.

I nodded as I looked at her. She was so young and so

far we hadn't seen anyone else with her. I had to hope her family was just out searching for food or helping survivors.

"He was, this is wonderful," I said when I swallowed my bite. "Is he still here? Are there others with you?"

She arched a brow and her eyes got sad and hard all at once. "No, there's no one left."

I shut my eyes and tried not to think of my own family. "Oh. How did it happen?"

She swallowed hard. "Yesterday one of the tour groups that come through this area came into the restaurant around lunchtime. We make a lot of money off those people, so my family is always excited when a bus parks outside our door. But one of the men with them had a bandage on his arm. He was acting weird and eventually he collapsed. Grandpa tried to help him but—"

She broke off, but we didn't need to hear her say it to know what had happened.

"The outbreak had already started by then, hadn't it? The tourist turned into a zombie and he bit your grandfather?" Dave whispered.

She seemed relieved not to have to recite those details herself. She nodded. "My Mom and my older brother rushed to help, but he got them before they knew what was happening."

"I'm sorry," I whispered as I looked at Dave from the corner of my eye.

"How did *you* keep from being turned, too?" he asked.

She looked at him like he was accusing her of something and her glare narrowed.

"I *wanted* to fight them," she snapped. "But my boyfriend forced me come up here. We bolted ourselves in and waited. We could hear them outside all night. Finally, this morning he couldn't take the way they were clawing at the door anymore. He took a shovel from the back deck and went down to deal with them." She swallowed hard. "He never came back. I finally dared to come down and found all these bodies. I shot some, bashed the heads in on others and stacked them up at the front door so the others wouldn't come in."

There was a long silence in the room. Finally, I shifted.

"I'm sorry," I repeated, though the sentiment seemed really stupid. "Uh, our friend got it this morning."

"I saw her body in your car when I walked by," Lisa said with a shrug. "It looks like she got shot in there, by one of you, after she turned."

Her eyes were really difficult to read and they were all I could see with her face covered by her mask, so I'm not sure if she was disgusted with us for killing Amanda or impressed that we had the guts.

I looked at Dave and he nodded like he read my mind.

"So how old are you?" Dave asked.

She turned her glare on him sharply. "Old enough."

"You can't be more than seventeen or eighteen," he pressed.

She folded her arms. "I'm *nineteen*. I graduated high school this year." She shifted slightly. "I was going to U-Dub in the fall. So was Alex. He is my ... well, he *was* my boyfriend."

We were all silent for a moment. I guess we were each thinking about what we'd lost in the last couple of days.

I had my own shit to deal with, but I couldn't imagine being ten years younger and on my own dealing with what was happening in the city around us.

Problems or not, at least I had David to depend on. And even though I was worried about my Dad down in San Diego and my Mom, who lived a couple of hours south of Chicago, so far there was no reason to believe they had been hurt. In fact, I knew my Dad had been okay as recently as yesterday afternoon when he e-mailed me. Probably they were both just scared out of their wits and wondering about my health and well-being.

This girl had lost her entire family, her boyfriend, her dreams, and her future in about thirty-six hours. Suddenly my life didn't seem so bad.

"We're on our way to the border, Longview, Washington," I offered awkwardly even though Lisa hadn't asked. "To find Dave's sister. If you want to come, you're welcome to ride along with us."

Dave nodded immediately and his hand settled on my knee under the table. He squeezed gently and I smiled at him. We might butt heads, but obviously we agreed on this point that the kid shouldn't be left alone like this. I was glad he didn't hesitate with her like he had with poor Amanda.

"So I'm some charity case for you?" she snapped as she grabbed the dirty plates and took them off the table.

Dave stared. "No, not at all. You'd be doing *us* a favor. We could use a third person to look out on the highway. And you're obviously a good shot and can take care of yourself."

From the sink, she eyed us for a minute, but then shook her head. "No way."

I got up and she stiffened. I saw her hand move toward the knife block behind her and I stopped moving immediately. "Why not, Lisa?"

"No offense but I don't know you two from Adam. You could be serial killers."

I stared at her. Under normal circumstances I would have been right there with her about not trusting people you just met. After all, my Mom had taught me not to take rides from strangers, too.

But this wasn't exactly "normal" anymore. Lisa was in the middle of a city basically overrun by zombies and she was alone. Not to mention a kid, for God's sake, no matter how well she was handling herself.

"But don't you want to get away from here?" Dave asked. "Seattle is going to be an undead town within a couple of days. You'll be trapped if you wait that long."

"Are you stupid enough to think it's going to be different somewhere else?" She glared at him. "You *have* been listening to the news, right?"

We glanced at each other and shifted uncomfortably. Since that morning, we'd been too busy trying not to die to turn on the radio. News wasn't a priority in comparison to battling for gas or having to kill a friend.

Lisa rolled her eyes.

"Okay, dumbasses, here's the news flash: this thing is *spreading*. By now there probably isn't even a Longview left. At least if I stay here I know where things are and I know how to get them." She folded her arms, an immovable object.

I sat back down at the table, totally stunned for a minute. I got that the outbreak was spreading, we could see that with our own eyes, but how could it have gotten so far so fast? Could it really be true that someplace a hundred and thirty miles away could be overrun already?

I shook my head. Even if what she said was true, we couldn't stop. We certainly couldn't stay here. I straightened my shoulders.

"Well, I guess that's true, but with more people in a group—"

"There's just more chance of getting turned into a zombie," Lisa finished with a dismissive sniff. "I mean, even your little headless friend out there you had to shoot in the end, right?" We didn't answer, but our silence seemed to satisfy her. She nodded. "Yeah, seeing her dead in your backseat doesn't really convince me that you two are my saviors."

Dave clenched his fists on the tabletop and I could tell he was thinking of that awful moment when he had to kill Amanda. This bitch might not know it, but she was rubbing that in.

"Look," I snapped, pissed off at her now. She was being a brat whether she knew it or not. "You're crazy to stay here alone."

She shook her head with a mocking and rather snotty little laugh. "Yeah? Well, I think *you're* crazy to stay together and try to run. You almost got turned in the car dealership today, lady. If I hadn't come along, you would have been eating your hubby here...and not in a good way. Could you have killed her, *Dave?*"

Dave got up and his chair rocked from how hard he'd pushed off. "Whatever, kid, you made your point. You want to stay here and rot, that's your choice. Thanks for the help back there, and for the food. We'll get out of your way."

I looked at him. "But—"

"Come on, Sarah," he said without looking away from the girl. "We're obviously not wanted here by the little girl who knows it all. So let's get going."

I got to my feet and started after him, but at the door that led downstairs to the restaurant, I looked back. Lisa had pulled her mask off and she was watching us leave. Her mouth was set in a stubborn line, but I saw the question in her eyes. The fear.

But she didn't stop us. And she didn't call us back.

We left the restaurant in silence and started back across the street together, each of us keeping an eye out for zombies.

"I don't get why she wouldn't come," I said in shock. "She's obviously not stupid or blind. She has to know she's dead if she doesn't make a break for it. She won't be able to hold them off forever."

Dave shrugged. "Who knows what she's thinking? Here she thinks she can control her environment. She's more afraid of the unknown than she is of having her arm chewed off by her former boyfriend when he pops back up from the dead. There wasn't going to be any convincing her to come. It was better to just get out of there before she decided we were too risky to let go."

My eyes widened. "You think she might have freaked out?"

"She looked like she might be heading that way," he said softly. "I saw her move for the knife when you got up. I wasn't going to take the chance."

I shivered. The idea that regular human people might try to hurt us hadn't actually occurred to me at that point. Oh, I was so innocent then. Luckily I didn't have to wrack my brain too hard about it because by then we were back in the parking lot of the dealership. The big fucking inflated gorilla waved in the breeze and I wanted to pop it with a big pin. I looked at the bloody show room where I'd almost lost my life half an hour earlier.

"I don't want to go back in there."

"We don't have to," Dave said. He held up a shiny key. "I grabbed one right before you got attacked."

He motioned toward a big black Escalade that was parked nearby. "I think *this* is your chariot, my lady."

I stared at the vehicle. It couldn't be more than a year old and it looked like whoever had owned it before it got to this lot had loved it like it was a kid.

The paint was perfectly shiny, not a scratch on her. Its big size would accommodate all our stuff and even a few more people if we found any more survivors who were actually willing to band together. And it could easily push smaller vehicles out of the way if need be.

"Perfect," I breathed. "Exactly what we wanted."

"Good," he said as he opened the passenger door and motioned me in. "Then let's pull her up to our car and move everything over."

Our car seemed small and really screwed up as we pulled the newer, fancier vehicle up next to it. Our old one was still smoking gently and I cringed at the pungent odor as I hopped down.

"You take the trunk," I said, "I'll grab everything out of the back."

He nodded and went around the car while I pulled the back door open. What I saw there made me stop and stare.

I knew Amanda was back there, of course. But seeing her slumped over at the oddest angle, a big exit wound through the back of her skull, made my stomach turn all over again. I couldn't move as I just *looked* down at her lifeless body. How the hell had we gotten to this?

Dave came around and stood beside me, both of us quiet for a long time.

"Come on," he finally said as he grabbed for one of the boxes of guns that were on the seat beside her, splattered with her blood, but still intact.

I nodded as I grabbed the other box and a couple of bags from our ill-fated gas station run. At the very least, I wasn't going to leave them and let her have died in vain.

We moved everything over to the new car and then we both looked at the old one.

"I don't want to leave her in the car," I said softly.

Dave looked at me. "Mandy?"

I nodded. "It seems wrong. Shouldn't we try to bury her or something? In the end, she was really brave, she saved our lives more than once. She even gave us permission to kill her so she wouldn't hurt us."

Dave stared at the car for a long time. "We can't take the time to bury her," he said quietly. "But we could burn the car."

I thought about that. "Cremation."

He nodded. "It's better than nothing, right?"

"Right."

Dave managed to siphon some gas out of the tank of Amanda's now make-shift coffin. Solemnly, he splashed it all over the car. I found a lighter hidden under the floor rug in the front seat from back when I still smoked...hey, I figured I might take it up again, might as well be ready. Dave pulled the new SUV away from the beater we'd been driving for four years and then I lit the lighter.

"Bye, Amanda," I whispered as I tossed it toward the busted-up car. "I'm really sorry."

The car ignited right away, the flames jumping high enough to singe tree branches ten feet above. I leaned away from the burst of heat and let out a sigh as Dave got out of the Escalade to stand beside me. We watched the car burn for a couple of minutes, lost in our thoughts.

And then I heard the sound. A low, echoing growl. Big, though, not the isolated sounds of the zombies like we'd heard before. I turned slightly and jerked back with a small scream.

Coming from around the back of the dealership were zombies. Maybe two hundred drooling, sludge-vomiting, growling zombies. They were a herd, that was the only way to describe them. Cattle on the stampede, and the two of us were their final destination if we didn't haul ass.

"They saw the smoke," I cried as I grabbed Dave and we dove for the new car. I crawled across to the passenger side from the driver's seat and he got in and slammed the door just as a dozen of the fastest-moving creatures reached the burning car.

Zombies are dumb. There, that's just the only thing you can say. Their brains are dead, or at least everything in their brain that makes them human and intelligent. So if a zombie sees fire, he doesn't go around it. He goes through it. And that's what about five of the fastest of them did.

As Dave gunned the engine and squealed out of the parking lot away from the horde of infected, I stared in horror at the flaming, lurching zombies who swarmed our old car before they started after us, completely oblivious to their searing flesh and burning clothes.

Dave pulled the vehicle onto the street between the lot and the back of the row of restaurants and I looked up. In the apartment window where we'd eaten with Lisa, I saw her face. It looked small on the second floor, watching the scene below as we rolled away.

I hoped we were right to leave her. Dave was correct, we couldn't have made her go. Still, I figured the chances of ever seeing her again were slim to none. So I shut my eyes and didn't look anymore until we were back on the highway.

CHAPTER 14

Listen. Killing zombies isn't easy.
There's bound to be fallout.

Although the road was still congested and it was slow going as we inched our way out of the downtown corridor toward the airport area fifteen miles away, we drove for a long time in total silence.

I think we were both too scared to turn on the radio after what Lisa had told us about the spread of the breakout. My brain was already overflowing with horror, I didn't think I could take much more.

And talking wasn't high on the 'to do' list, either. Both of us were thinking about scary, awful things and I'm not sure we trusted each other enough to share them.

I know, for my part, I just kept thinking about Amanda. About her innocence and her unexpected bravery... about the awful moments leading to her death. And by the way Dave's jaw was set and the dire expression on his face, I knew he was thinking those same things, too. And maybe wishing he hadn't been so tough on her before she died.

Dr. Kelly had once called Dave a "brooder." She'd

explained that he kept his thoughts inside and that some-times it was better to talk them out. At the time that had elicited an eye roll from me, but I couldn't help but think about it now as I looked at him.

Finally, I blurted out, "We had to kill her."

For a long time, Dave's flinch was the only answer. When he spoke, his voice was strained. "Well, *we* didn't kill her in committee or something. I killed her."

"David—" I started, kind of scared by how hollow his voice was. He sounded really fucked up. The same way he had the day he told me he was dropping out of school and we had fought for three hours.

"No," he snapped and his sharp tone cut me off. "I should have checked the bathroom. Why didn't I fucking check the bathroom?"

With a yell, he slammed both palms against the steer-ing wheel. The car veered slightly and we almost hit an old truck that was angled into the shoulder, but he man-aged to pull the Escalade back into a straight line before he wrecked it. More than I could manage, as you already know.

He was breathing hard as he continued to drive. Care-fully, I reached out and I touched his arm. He didn't pull away, so I patted him gently.

I thought about what he'd said to me in the garage earlier that morning. About how we didn't know what we were doing, but we were trying our best in a bad situa-tion. I hoped those same words might help him now.

"*We* didn't check the bathroom because we're new at this," I said.

He glared at me from the corner of his eye. "What?"

"I said we're new at this. I mean, it's not like they

teach you how to survive a zombie attack in school." I shivered. Maybe now they would. "We're still learning what we need to do to protect ourselves and anyone else who rides with us. Next time we're in a similar situation, I guess we'll know better. We'll always check the bathroom from now on."

"Next time," Dave said, coughing out a bitter laugh. "How ridiculous is it that we know a next time is coming?"

I didn't answer. Of course there was going to be a next time. I'd already accepted that as an inevitability.

He rubbed his chin. "But some good our little learning experience does Amanda."

"I know," I whispered, blinking back tears.

"She was like a little kid," he muttered.

I looked at him. "And *that* wasn't your fault, either."

"But I should have—"

I squeezed his hand. "David, Amanda was twenty-three. Old enough to be careful in this situation. So don't take all the credit or the blame for her survival or her death. We did the best we could. It sucks, but we can't beat ourselves up. We've killed plenty of people we know."

Dave was quiet for a minute, but then he started laughing. I stared at him, hoping he hadn't lost his mind since he was driving and I didn't relish the idea of trying to find another car if he wrecked, this time on a zombie-infested freeway.

"I bet you never thought you'd be saying that," Dave said as he continued to laugh.

I smiled despite myself. "Yeah, I guess not."

"'We've killed plenty of people we know,'" he chuckled, mimicking my voice.

I have to say, I hated when he did that, but today I didn't take it personally. I actually laughed along with him.

"Well, we *have*. Let's see, there was our debut with Dr. Kelly."

"Who overcharged us for advice I could have gotten on a fortune cookie," Dave said.

I giggled. "That's as good a reason to kill her as the fact that she was going to eat us."

"The Wonderful Wilsons," he offered.

"Technically, we didn't kill them," I reminded him. "But they were posers and I think they liked to rub it in when they came out of Dr. Kelly's office every week. I can't be sorry for them."

"Total posers," he agreed. "How about Jack?"

I hesitated. Jack had been David's friend, even if I despised him. Maybe I shouldn't kid about him, it might be a sorer subject than my husband let on.

"Oh, come on, don't stop now," Dave encouraged with a wicked little grin. "I *know* you wanted to beat him to death in the toilet for way more than one thing."

"Wellll," I dragged out the word.

"Here, I'll start." Dave took a deep breath like he was about to confess something really bad. "Jack cheated at Halo. In fact, he cheated at all video games."

"What?" I asked, turning toward him. "He did not."

"He did. I caught him at it a hundred times." He winked. "Now you."

"Okay, he also played his music too loud on week-nights and he smelled like sausage," I said, covering my mouth as I said it.

"Sentence: Death!" David snorted. "Mr. Gonzales is obvious."

I rolled my eyes. "Too easy. Jackass, looked at my tits, refused to fix anything, total slumlord."

"And I guess that just leaves us back to Amanda," he said with a sigh.

I looked at him, still feeling bad no matter how much we both tried to lighten the mood.

"A cheerleader was mean to me in high school," I said after a long pause. "And Amanda always reminded me of her. So I guess that's a good enough reason for a rampage. In reality, you were defending my honor."

He smiled. "Yeah. I'll take that."

"So we're good?" I asked. "We've confessed our sins and said our Hail Marys and we're okay to kill again?"

He nodded. "But now I guess it's time to do the thing we've been avoiding and listen to some news. We better see what kind of situation the rest of the world is in."

I turned the stereo dial and the awesome speakers blasted a woman talking. I looked at the display and smiled, "Heyyyy, satellite. I've always wanted satellite radio!"

"I know. It's part of why I picked this one. I mean, Playboy radio, Howard Stern." He waggled his eyebrows suggestively and relief washed over me. Dave was going to be okay.

I gave his arm a light slap. "Pervert."

I flipped the dial until it read MSNBC on the dial and turned it up as a female reporter with a lightly British accent talked in a calm and even tone.

"Officials have abandoned the city, with one anonymous source telling us it is 'left to God' now. But as the disease spreads unabated, with more and more undead popping up in almost every West Coast city, there are increasing questions about whether local, state, and federal forces are equipped to deal with what scientists are now saying will soon be a global plague."

"Shit, she was right," I murmured, thinking of Lisa walled into her tower trying to will the zombies away. I hoped she was okay even if she was a bitch.

"While officials do stand by their suggestion that people stay in their homes, they also tell those who do venture out to arm themselves and aim for the head if they come in contact with one of the infected. Those who are bitten seem to have between ten and twenty-five minutes until they are fully transformed, depending upon body chemistry and the location of the bite. There is no known cure—"

I turned the volume down. That was enough for now.

"Lisa might be right after all," Dave said in a low, sad tone. "Longview might be no better than Seattle by now."

I shrugged. "I don't care. That's our plan. I say we stick to it. At least it gives us something to aim for. Once we get there, we'll figure out what to do next."

He nodded and then we drove, back into silence as we both tried to figure out what the hell we'd gotten ourselves into.

CHAPTER 15

Support your partner in their interests. You never know when batting practice, kung fu movie moves, or even a poker night might come in handy during a zombie infestation.

We hadn't even reached the airport when the sun started to set. Both of us had been watching it droop lower and lower on the horizon during the hours of dodging cars and crushing zombies along the shoulder of the freeway. The entire afternoon I kept hoping some miracle would happen and we'd somehow hit the open road and have a straight shot to Longview.

Of course it didn't.

"We won't make it before dark," Dave said with a sigh.

I nodded without looking at him. "I guess we'll have to stop."

I sent him a side glance and saw how thin and pissed his mouth was. He wasn't any happier about this than I was. "Unless you want to take your chances on the road at night."

He shook his head immediately. "I thought about it.

There are just too many cars and way too many zombies. I think it would be a deathtrap."

I didn't answer as I started looking out the car window at the area we were in. We were out of Seattle proper by now so there were no longer skyscrapers, but all the little suburbs were so tight in and crowded that we were still in the city in every way that mattered. There were still tons of people out there, tons of cars, tons of opportunities for death...and undeath.

I scanned for a place out in the hilly neighborhoods of businesses and homes for a location that looked safe. It's funny how much you take "safe" for granted until it's gone. How many road trips had we been on when we'd just grabbed a room at a Super 8 without even thinking about it? I even used to complain about crappy towels or cheap sheets, which drove David nuts. But I'd kill for them at this point if it meant we didn't have to battle any more zombies to get them.

"Hmmm," I muttered as we meandered past a part of the highway where I could see a neighborhood with homes built down on the hill below. They were squeezed close together like sardines. "Maybe a house would be a good pick. If we could break in—"

"Nope," Dave interrupted as he eased the car toward the next off ramp. "I know exactly where we're going to go."

I wrinkled my brow. How did he know any better than I did where the safest place to stop was? It wasn't like we came down here more than a couple times a year for airport runs when one of our sets of parents came.

"Where?" I asked, totally incredulous.

"You'll see..." he teased as he drove along what was

once a main thoroughfare but now abandoned cars lined the lanes.

A Laundromat to one side of the street was on fire, the chemicals within making the flames purple and blue. On the other side there was an antique store with all its windows broken out, only from the inside, not the outside. The shards of broken glass still pointing up from the frame and sparkling in the sunset were tinged with both blood and sludge.

Basically, it was a ghost town.

Suddenly on our left I saw the flashing, garish, neon lights of a sign. "Sea King Hotel and Casino." The "K" was shorted out, so that it only buzzed faintly.

I turned in my seat and stared at David as he pulled into the half-empty lot in front of the casino and parked.

"Have you lost your fucking mind?"

He glared at me. "Um, no. Haven't we always joked that we need to come down here and bet all our savings on red? It seems like this is as good a time as ever."

"Okay, clearly this zombie thing has broken your brain," I snapped as I folded my arms. "Yes, we talked about that, but a) that was a *joke* and b) it was before the world freaking imploded and monsters starting rising from the dead."

He tilted his head. "But we're right here. How could it hurt to look?"

"Are you serious?" I motioned toward the two story building a hundred yards across the lot. "Let's see . . . it's a public place where lots of people were potentially turned into zombies. It's also a place where there was money and freaky looters could have decided this was their time to clear the tables. If they see us as a threat . . ." I pulled my thumb along my throat in a slashing motion. "You ran out on Lisa for a lot less!"

Dave scowled and his tone was a warning when he said, "Sarah—"

But I wasn't done yet. Not by a long shot. "Also, it's a huge place, doesn't the sign say over one hundred rooms? That means one hundred areas we can't check. Shall I go on?"

Dave shook his head. "I know all that. But Sarah, finding that girl in Seattle made me think about *other* people who might be out there like her. And not all of them are going to be too scared to make a run for it. If we just had a couple more people helping us to shoot and to drive, we might have a better chance at survival."

I shook my head. "You're right, there may be people here, but—"

"Fuck, Sarah!" he said, gripping the steering wheel until his knuckles went white. "Do you have to argue about *every fucking thing*?"

"I don't—"

"Yes, you do." He faced me. "For six months you've been telling me every single thing and every way I've fucked up. And I've *let* you."

I flinched because the way he was describing me wasn't fun. But hell, I'd been the one to have to deal with the consequences of his choices. Didn't I have a right to question them?

He set his head on the steering wheel for a minute, drawing some deep breaths before he looked at me.

"Look, if you really think I'm such a colossal idiot, if you don't trust me and you don't want to go in there with me . . . then maybe you should just take the car and go."

"Yes, we should take the car and go," I said with a sigh of relief. Finally, he was being reasonable.

He shook his head. "No. I said *you*, not we."

There was a long silence while I let that sink in. He wasn't talking about taking a break. He wasn't even talking about me looking for someplace else to stay and coming back to pick him up after he'd checked out this place and had his fill of poker tables and cocktail waitress zombies.

He was talking about *us* being done. Finished.

"You-you want me to leave?" I said. Well, I whispered it, really. I couldn't seem to talk louder than that.

He reached out and his hands cupped my shoulders. "No, honey, I want you to stay. But not if we're going to keep doing this."

I stared at him. I'd never seen him like this. Even with Dr. Kelly poking and prodding for "honesty" during therapy he'd never been so frank.

"I know I've fucked up," he whispered. "When I quit school and went off the grid it screwed up all our plans. It put all the pressure of our lives on you to bear because I didn't know who I was or what to do anymore. Trust me, I know *everything* that I did wrong and I think I've hated myself almost as much as you've hated me. But you can't punish me forever, right?"

I blinked, still stunned. He let me go and unbuckled his seatbelt with a sigh. I watched his every move as he got out and closed the door behind him. He walked around the front of the car, his gun ready as he looked around for zombies. At my door, he stopped and opened it.

"Now, are you coming or going?" he asked, holding the door open for me.

The question broke my spell. Nodding, I grabbed for my own shotgun, stuck a handgun in my pant waist and got out.

"Coming," I said as I shut the door behind me.

He clicked the AUTO LOCK button on the door and then he reached for my hand. As I took it, he smiled.

"Good. Because this is probably going to be messed up."

He was right. It was messed up. When we entered the building, both of us wrinkled our noses and stared in stunned disbelief. The casino had been built probably in the sixties or seventies, when Frank Sinatra and his Rat Pack were swinging in Vegas and making hip, cool cats want to play their hand at roulette and high stakes blackjack while they sipped martinis and made passes at broads.

But since those times the place hadn't been updated, so instead of being cool or even kitschy, it was run down. The once red carpet at the entryway was worn with holes and dotted with stains and it had faded to a salmon pink...except in the spots where blood had dried it.

But *those* updates were recent.

All the walls had black marks where things had rubbed against them over the years. The dirt was noticeable, the mold around the corners disturbing and the splashes of black sludge and flecks of flesh and brains that marred the yellowing white paint...well, they were telling.

A registration desk for guests of the hotel was off to the left, but activity with the infected had obviously continued here because blood was slashed across the wall behind the counter, including on the cracked screen of a dingy television that was half-pulled out of the wall. It dangled precariously just by its connection to the cable outlet behind it while its shredded electric cord sparked and smoked faintly.

We exchanged a brief look and raised our guns at the same time before we moved onto the main casino floor with its colorful flashing machines and big, empty tables.

To my surprise, there were still people sitting at the slot machines, pulling the handles methodically. Although they were mostly blue-haired old ladies frittering away their social security checks, there were also some really fantastic bits of trailer trash mixed in. Men with huge guts, leather vests, and two-foot-long pony tails, and middle-aged women with pierced belly buttons and huge tattoos on their saggy boobs.

I guess the place just attracted the most pathetic clientele in the city. People who didn't care, or maybe even know, that the world was coming to an end outside these gross, dismal walls.

At least that's what I *thought*. Until we actually got closer. And that's when I realized that the little old women at the slots weren't human anymore. Their skin was grey, sludge smeared the screens of their machines and they groaned and muttered in that zombie way under their breath even as they yanked on the slot handles with a never-ending rhythm.

"Shit," I whispered, grabbing Dave's arm and pointing wildly at the closet one, who looked like she had been about ninety before she received the huge bite that I now noticed on her wrinkled, dropping neck.

He stared at her and then at the others, his eyes as wide as I'm sure mine were.

"Well," he whispered. "I guess we know now that *this* particular activity doesn't require higher brain function. I wonder what else zombies can do in their spare time."

"I don't care about what they can do," I hissed in his ear, still clinging to his arm. "What do *we* do? Should we fight them?"

He looked around the casino floor while he pondered that question and then he shook his head. "No, I don't think so. I mean, look at how many people are on these machines."

I followed his gesture out across the floor and counted over twenty people tugging slots.

"We have to assume everyone out there is a zombie."

"They might not be," I said, more as a hopeful statement than a secure one.

He speared me with a look. "Come on, Sarah. Even the biggest gambling addict would *have* to notice if zombies attacked the guy next to them. And if they didn't, if they were *so* caught up in what they were doing that they didn't try to fight, that would just make them better targets for the infected."

I nodded. "Okay, okay, that makes sense. So they're all zombies."

"I'm afraid if we fired on one, it would wake the rest of them up from this gambling stupor and we'd end up with God knows how many undead rushing us from all sides." Dave shook his head. "With just the two of us to fight and so few weapons, I think we'd be screwed."

"So what then?" I asked, edging away as the slot machine that the zombie in front of us was sitting at suddenly dinged loudly and dropped a payout into its bin.

The grandma zombie whined and looked down at the tokens as they clattered against each other in her bin. She hesitated, then drew one from the bin and popped it back into the slot machine to continue her run at riches. Not that a zombie would have any use for them.

"We could sneak by since they're so caught up. I mean this one could care less we're standing here," Dave said with a shrug.

I should have listened to my gut, which was telling me to make a run for it and get back in the car. But Dave had scared me so badly when he said we should part ways that I was determined to prove to him that I wasn't going to argue with him about every decision.

So instead of backing out, I said, "I guess there could be people in the back rooms like the kitchen and that kind of thing. There are a lot of areas here to search before we give up on survivors entirely."

He nodded and I think he was relieved that we were on the same side for once.

"If we could find others...we would be safer. I mean, every time you got out of the SUV to clear out a car today, I was so scared you were going to get hurt. With one or two people to cover you..."

I stared at him as he trailed off. So all this was for *me*? To protect me? And a bunch of warm feelings I hadn't felt for him in a long time swelled up in me: Pride. Love. Comfort.

It was nice. And I wanted him to know it.

"You're brave," I whispered.

He shrugged, but beyond his discomfort and the way his cheeks turned beet red, I know what I said meant something to him.

"Well, somebody has to be the hero like in those books you read," he said with a dismissive shrug.

I smiled as I followed him toward a doorway that led to the kitchen in the back of the casino floor. I don't think he heard me when I whispered, "You are."

CHAPTER 16

Talk openly about important issues like money, sex, and religion. They can affect your life and happiness a great deal. Especially when it comes to cults.

The kitchen door was one of those that swing in and out. David pushed it open and caught it with one hand as it came back toward him.

We peeked in. The kitchen was a large, industrial one with shining metal counters and cabinets, but it was anything but clean. The faint smell of rotting food wafted toward us from the piles of meat and vegetables that had obviously been in the process of preparation when the infection hit this part of the city. I looked at the flies buzzing around a piece of beef and my stomach turned. It reminded me too much of rotting zombie flesh. Weird because I'd lost my gag reflex when it came to them within a few hours of the outbreak.

"It looks clear," Dave whispered as he slipped inside and motioned me to follow.

I moved into the space and started to come around

beside him, but he put an arm out and blocked me, keeping me behind him.

"Just in case," he whispered. "Now call out."

I tilted my head in confusion. "Call out?"

He nodded with utter certainty. "If someone's hiding in here, they might be less afraid if a woman calls for them than a man."

I rolled my eyes but since I didn't want to argue the concept of feminism with my husband at that particular moment, I cleared my throat.

"Is anyone there?" I called. "If you're a survivor, please come out. We might be able to help you."

There was no answer. I looked toward Dave with a shrug but he motioned his head as if encouraging me to try again.

"Hello?" I said, this time louder, though I didn't think there was any point. "Is anyone there?"

Dave shrugged. "Okay, I guess—"

Before he could finish, I grabbed his arm. In the distance, I heard a sliding sound. As we stood there, it came again. It seemed to emanate from the large walk-in freezer across the wide expanse of the kitchen.

"Did you hear that?" I asked as I motioned toward the unit with my hand.

Dave nodded and we moved forward together, checking around us down the kitchen corridors and through the metal shelving for any people...or zombies...who might be hiding.

But there was nothing to be seen or found until we reached the metal doors of the freezer. I leveled my gun as Dave reached out and gently turned the handle of the fridge. He pulled the door open slowly. A blast of frigid air hit us and we both flinched back from the cold.

Inside the freezer was dark. I could see the outline of a bulb at the top of it from the light of the kitchen, but it was broken.

Broken.

"David, I think it might be—" I started.

Before I could finish a zombie rushed from the unit. If he hadn't been so terrifying, I might have laughed at the sight. He wore a white chef's jacket that had once been pristine, but was now covered with black vomit. His skin was blue-grey from the cold and his dark hair was filled with ice particles, including little icicles in his eyelashes that made his red pupils all the more pronounced.

All those things made him look ridiculous, but I couldn't find it funny because he lunged so quickly at Dave that he was on him before I could fire my weapon and the two of them staggered backward and fell to the floor.

The zombie bit at my husband and it was only because David jerked his head to the side that he wasn't turned to the ranks of the undead. I flipped my gun around and swung, crushing the butt of it against the zombie's temple. He fell off of David and rolled away across the white kitchen floor with a furious growl of pain and aggression.

I shoved the butt of the gun against my shoulder and began to depress the trigger. But before I fired, a machete came flipping through the air and struck the zombie in the back of the skull. He whined softly and then the light went out of his red eyes.

I spun in the direction the machete had flown from to find a man standing in the doorway we had entered the kitchen from. He looked to be about thirty-five, with shoulder-length blond hair and a surprisingly serene expression on his face, as if none of this really bothered him. I wasn't sure if it was shellshock, but it wasn't normal.

"I wouldn't fire a gun in here if I were you," he said, his voice calm and smooth as silk. "The sound will bring the rest running."

"Look out!" I cried before I could say anything else, because from the walk-in fridge where the first zombie had come, two more were on their way out, jerking toward our now-unarmed savior.

I flipped my shotgun around, taking into account what the stranger had said about not firing and swung, bringing the butt down right on the crown of the first zombie's skull. It hit with a thunk and a splat, almost like you'd see during the "fights" in the old Batman series...only in my version the skull cracked like a melon, spraying brains, blood, and flesh in all directions.

Dave was on his feet behind me as I took care of the lead zombie. He yanked the newcomer's machete from the skull of the chef zombie who had attacked him and with a slicing motion right out of a video game, decapitated the zombie straggler. His head bounced like a basketball on the linoleum floor before it rolled away under the metal shelving.

The newcomer nodded toward us, a smile on his otherwise calm face. "I am much obliged to you, I'm sure," he said as he stepped into the room.

I gasped in shock because three others stood behind him. Humans! Uninfected, a man and two women. They stared at me, then toward Dave with curiously blank expressions. Apparently this guy had had back-up all the time. He didn't need our help, I guess.

"I'll take that," the man said, holding out his hand toward David, who stood staring at the small group, his mouth dropped open in shock and the bloody machete still dripping in his hand.

"What?" he said with a shake of his head. The other man motioned toward the weapon and David nodded. "Oh yes, of course."

He took the machete and casually wiped the blade on the closest zombie's shredded shirt and then slipped it into a big sheath fastened at his waist.

"Th-thank you," Dave finally said as he extended a hand. "You certainly saved us."

Unlike when we had met Lisa in Seattle and she had refused our attempts at friendship, this man immediately clasped hands with David.

"Not at all," he said. "We *saved* each other. And we always welcome more soldiers in God's war against the unclean."

My brow wrinkled. David and I are not religious people, okay. I think by now you probably guessed that. Sunday was my only day off, so I'd much rather sleep in and make pancakes than go sit in a stuffy church and get preached at by a bunch of hypocrites, but I respected other people's right to religion. And I guess under these circumstances some people find a lot of comfort in their faith.

I figured this guy must be one of them and I held my hand out.

"I'm Sarah."

"Sarah," he repeated with a smile. He took my hand

and held it in both of his instead of shaking it. His palms were warm and slightly humid. "My name is William Blackwell."

I nodded as I pulled to free my hand. He let me go, but only after a slight struggle on my part.

"And there are four of you here," I said, sliding closer to Dave and putting my arm around him without thinking about why. "That's wonderful. We haven't seen so many survivors since the outbreak started yesterday."

William smiled, but I sort of felt like he was looking at a little kid who needed a complicated idea explained. There was condescension in his gaze that irritated me.

"Oh, there are far more than four of us left," he said in that same soft monotone he had used when warning me against firing the gun.

Dave squeezed my waist and I felt the excitement move through him almost like electricity. "More! Wow, that's wonderful. We're so happy to have found you. See Sarah, I told you there might be people here."

I nodded, unable to keep my eyes off the man before us. "Yeah, you were right on that one."

William smiled. "Why don't you come along with us? We'll let you meet the others."

I blinked, overcome by disbelief. "You mean, they're here? Close by?"

He nodded. "Oh yes, many others just a few steps away."

For the first time in days, hope swelled inside of me. Many others right here, like a camp or something! Had they come here after the outbreak or merely banded together when the attack began in the casino?

Oh, it didn't matter. The very idea that there was a group of survivors after so many pieces of bad news and so many disappointments made me think we could make it to Longview after all. Hell, I was even starting to think we could find my parents or Dave's.

"Come." William motioned toward the door.

Dave and I walked toward the others and I peeked over my shoulder. William was walking behind me with a slow, steady gait while the others with him moved before us. I felt like we were being led somewhere. It wasn't comfortable, but I was still so twitterpated with the concept of other survivors that I ignored my intuition.

We wound down some hallways behind the casino floor until we reached a back ballroom. There was a sign outside the door. You know, the kind hotels print up at conferences or for other meetings? Well, this one said, BLACKWELL TRUTH CHURCH GROUP. I frowned as one of the women pulled the door open and motioned us inside.

I suck at remembering names, but I was pretty damned certain that Blackwell was what William had told us his name was a few minutes earlier. But "Truth Church Group"? That sounded like someplace that asked for money in exchange for salvation on TV.

Before I could ask for more details, we stepped into the room and I staggered back at what I saw. At the far side of the ballroom were probably thirty people. There were women who were all dressed in mid-calf dresses and a handful of wussy-looking men with pale skin and soft jaws. There were even a few children either held in the arms of their mothers or big enough to stand in small groups of their own. Their long faces were filled with fear and doubt.

They turned, almost as a herd, as we came in. They had the same blank looks of the three others accompanying William. The ones who were now standing behind us at the door, as if guarding it, though now I wasn't so sure if that was to keep zombies out... or keep these people in.

Immediately, William stepped in front of us and said, "Brothers and sisters, we've been privileged to find more sheep for our flock. Others who have survived the wrath of God's hand and battled the unclean who wait like wolves outside these very doors."

A murmur worked its way through the crowd and William smiled like he was enjoying his own show.

"Welcome Sarah and David," he finished.

"Ah," said a woman, stepping forward.

She was wearing a long dress and her dark hair was pulled back into a bun. From the size of it, I figured her hair must reach past her ass when it was down. Also, she didn't have that blank look of the others. No, this woman looked sharp as a whip.

She shot William a knowing look as she held out her hands. "We always welcome fellow soldiers to the war. And ones with such good, Christian names. I'm Melissa Blackwell, William's wife."

I blinked. The bad feeling that had started in my stomach before we entered the kitchen and grown when William started talking about God and stuff was now screaming at me.

"Er, well I'm not sure about the soldiers part," Dave murmured, his tone telling me he was as squigged out by this as I was. "Just people who were lucky enough to survive this tragedy."

"We don't believe in luck," William said as he put his arm around the woman with the long hair. "Melissa and I believe in fate. The destiny Our Lord presents to us. After all, there is a reason that our church group decided to come to this place to meet at this time."

I stared. So this group had been here at the time of the breakout? It seemed odd for a church group to decide to meet in a place like this, surrounded by vice of all kinds.

I looked around. "Was it the low rates? Let me guess, it was the table games?"

His smile, that ever-present benign smile that matched his even tone so perfectly, faltered a little at my sarcasm. "No, child, we chose this place because where better to face sinners than on their own heartland?"

"A casino," Dave said slowly.

He nodded. "Yes, brother. This place was already the devil's playground. And the Lord sent his vengeance down upon it with merciless precision. He turned all those who walked in Satan's shadow into the unclean, the monsters you have seen outside."

I shook my head. "N-No. You don't understand. That didn't just happen here, it's actually happening everywhere, Mr. Blackwell."

"Father William," he said, turning toward me. "Please."

Yeah, I wasn't about to call him that. Instead, I continued with a shake of my head.

"We came from Seattle and the infestation has happened all across the city and even beyond it, if the news reports are correct."

His face lit up and in that moment my entire body tensed. He actually seemed *happy* to hear that news. He turned to his followers and said, "Did you hear that, brothers and sisters! God's vengeance is coming down in Seattle, a city of sin, indeed."

I stared as the men and women started praising the Lord at this news. The idea that the city had been all but wiped out by this horrible infestation actually excited them and they raised their hands and waved them around.

I grabbed Dave's arm gently to get his attention because he seemed as mesmerized as I was by what was happening right before us. He slowly lowered his head and our eyes met. In his gaze, I saw the same disgust, the same abject horror as I felt in that moment.

"David," I whispered, watching the group start a prayer in the background. "Um...I think this is a cult."

He didn't answer, he just stared.

"We're so happy to have you join us," Melissa said to us after William's prayer of joy at "God's Vengeance" was finished. "I know you'll be right at home with our flock within a few days."

She grabbed my arm. I guess it was meant as a comforting gesture, but her nails dug into my skin and it felt more like she was holding me where I was.

"I think you've misunderstood," Dave said, taking my other arm. Now I was trapped between them and neither one seemed to want to let go. "We aren't planning to stay. Sarah and I are headed for family in Longview. We only planned to stop here for a night."

I noticed he didn't invite any of these weirdos to join us on our trip, even though that had been our hope when we tried to find other people.

William turned on us and the murmured prayers of the surrounding people died with a collective gasp.

"Oh no," he said. "You cannot go. God brought you to us for a reason."

"Look, I don't mean to disrespect your beliefs, William, but the neon sign led us here, not God," Dave said, and I could see he was freaked out and pissed off and trying to rein it all in.

He was doing pretty well, too. The only reason I knew what was going on in his head was because we'd been together so long.

William, on the other hand, couldn't hide his rage as he turned on my husband with the fire and brimstone of a rabid preacher.

"Don't blaspheme," he snapped, his hands fisting at his sides and his eyes widening. "Or deny God or you'll be stricken by this plague, David."

Both of us recoiled. That sounded like a threat, not a statement. At that moment my brain exploded with possibilities. Had there been others who had refused this "offer"? Had they been left to the zombies outside? Maybe even those poor fools in the kitchen...

Dave leaned closer. "With *your* help, I assume," he said, his teeth clenched.

I stepped between them and turned toward William, though I reached back to take Dave's hand and squeezed gently.

"We wouldn't dare question your beliefs," I said, keeping my voice low so we wouldn't cause a riot. These were people on the edge. I recognized it now in the wildness of their expressions. "But my husband and I have been through a great deal over the last two days and we *are* going to Longview to see if our family is all right. We certainly appreciate your hospitality in allowing us to stay with your group tonight, but tomorrow we intend to continue on our path."

"Oh no," Melissa said. She was smiling but it didn't even come close to reaching her eyes. "You *must* stay with us. You see, we've been saved, spared from this plague and now we are called by God to draw all the survivors to us. You are part of our family now."

I opened my mouth but William interrupted. "It is our duty to repopulate the earth."

I swallowed. When he said that, he was looking at me. From top to bottom like he was checking out a great steak. I thought about all the shows I'd watched over the years on cults. Didn't their leaders always... *mate* with their followers? They wanted to own all the children, claim all the females.

"And now," William said, his tone increasingly menacing, "I think we'll be taking your weapons."

Dave tensed behind me. "What? No fucking way are we giving you our guns."

The group that had been milling around benignly in the distance suddenly moved forward. I stared. They almost seemed like zombies, moving as a group, their eyes blank. But they were human. This was human herd mentality.

And just like the zombies, it was dangerous and terrifying.

"David," I whispered.

He looked toward the group and his face paled. "You can't leave us defenseless."

William smiled. "Oh, you won't be defenseless. You'll be with us and that means you'll be with God. But just remember, the Lord giveth, David. And the Lord can taketh away."

CHAPTER 17

Plan romantic getaways. Or just getaways.

One thing I can say about the Sea King Hotel and Casino is that they had far nicer rooms than I'd expected when we walked in the door hours before. They weren't great, don't get me wrong, but I had some really *low* expectations based on the shitty appearance of the lower level. Now that we were in a room, I couldn't complain much. It was clean with two queen-sized beds and a little desk by the window.

Unfortunately, at the moment, those rooms were our prison, so I had less appreciation for them than I would have if we'd just come to stay for a weekend excursion.

Dave handed over a cracker and a slice of cheese that he was forced to hack off with a plastic knife. Yeah, our cult-y captors had given us food, but they'd decided we couldn't even be trusted with a steak knife. It was like the airlines, but without the instructions for what to do in an emergency. Right now, we could have used them.

I crunched on the cracker as I cast a side glance at the hotel door. I had already checked through the peephole a couple of times since some of William and Melissa's minions had tossed us into a room (not even a suite, the cheapskates).

What I'd seen every time I checked were guards standing outside. And not just any guards, but two of the biggest followers in the group armed with wicked machetes that they held like they'd been training for this moment. The worst part was...maybe they had.

I wasn't about to tangle with them one way or another, especially without any weapons of our own.

"Okay, are we going to talk about this?" Dave sighed.

"Talk about what?" I asked before I chugged some water from the mini-bar. "There's so much to cover here."

He laughed softly. "Yeah, but I meant talk about *them*."

"You mean asshole and assholette?" When David nodded, I shook my head. "We never should have saved that shithead. We could have let the zombies in the kitchen get him."

He grinned, but it was tense. "I admit the idea of watching him get eaten alive is pretty pleasant right now, but there was no way we could have known that at the time."

I shrugged. "Yeah, you hardly ever come face to face with a genuine—" I dropped my voice to a whisper, in case *they* were listening outside to report back to William and Melissa about what we were saying, "—cult."

"Yeah," he said with a frown.

I nodded. "I guess we've got to figure out what to do

next, as much as I'd like to pretend like none of this is happening. But we *are* in the middle of a zombie out-break, we're trying to get another hundred miles plus to your sister's... and we've just been taken hostage by a crazy-ass cult that thinks this zombie thing is the hand of God. Ignoring the problem—er, *problems*—is clearly not going to fix them."

"Nice summary," Dave said as he got to his feet and brushed cracker bits from his pants. "Right now I think the zombies are the least of our worries."

"I never thought we'd say that," I said with a shake of my head. "But you're right, at least for now."

I shivered as I thought of the dead eyes of Blackwell's followers. They were such a stark contrast to the bright intelligence of his and his wife's. Unlike the zombies, those two knew exactly what they were doing. And if we got in the way, we wouldn't make it. They would make sure of that.

"We have to get out of here." I rubbed my eyes. "As soon as we possibly can."

"I think tonight is our best chance." Dave paced the room to the window and turned back. His hands were clenched at his sides. "I saw how he looked at you when he talked about repopulating the earth."

I shrugged. "Isn't that typical cult behavior? From all the documentaries I've ever watched on the subject, it seems like the leaders always manipulate the women into marrying them or sleeping with them or whatever."

Dave spun around and I could see how pissed he was from the way his shoulders and back hunched. I have to admit, I kind of liked this chest-banging-woman-mine thing that was going on with him. It was sort of a new experience from Mr. Laid Back, Play a Videogame Dude.

"Well, I'm not letting that happen to you," he said without looking at me.

I shook my head as I thought about the cult again. "The thing that bothers me is how in the world did these people get so crazy so fast? This outbreak only started yesterday."

He shrugged, still not looking at me, but outside. "They were already crazy. I mean, you saw that sign outside the ballroom! 'Blackwell Truth Church'... these people were already spouting nonsense. This whole situation just gives them the excuse they were looking for to carry out some kind of manifesto. It's like Jonestown or those comet people from a few years ago."

I swallowed. All those people in the cults he was talking about had ended up dead. And they hadn't had an imminent threat of zombies right outside their doors to ramp up their mass hysteria.

"Well, how do we get away?" I asked. "There are guards at the door. And there's no reasoning with good old Bill and Mel, down there."

He turned slowly. "We aren't going to reason. We're just going to run."

"How?" I asked, then looked toward the door and lowered my voice again.

He jerked his thumb toward the window and arched a brow. I hurried over to his side and looked out. The sun was pretty much down now and the world was frighteningly dark outside, but there were still some parking lot and exterior lights. In their glow, I could see that our room was just above the awning that hung over the casino entrance.

I turned back toward him with wide eyes and my first feeling of hope since our capture. "Holy shit, Dave! It's only about what...ten feet down from here to there?"

He nodded. "And another short drop to the ground after that. I think we can make it. William took the keys to the Escalade, but I'll bet at least one of these cars in the lot has keys in the ignition from when the owner was attacked. If we're lucky, we'll spot one right away and we can make a break for it."

I shivered. "But...but there are zombies out there," I whispered as I stared again into the looming darkness where real monsters roamed looking for flesh.

He put his arm around me as we stared out into the unknown abyss. "Yes, that's very true. And it's going to be dangerous, I won't lie to you. But I'm pretty sure if we stay here that these crazy people are going to hurt us just as badly as any zombie could. In fact, maybe worse. I'll take my chances on the open road."

I nodded. His words were creeping past my fears. Worming into my brain. I had argued with him about a lot of things and a lot of decisions, but this time there was nothing to say. He was right.

"You know, I almost feel sorry for the zombies," I mused as we stared out at the parking lot that could mean our freedom. "They kill for food...for base needs. They're like an animal. They have no choice."

Dave shrugged. "I don't know if I'd go so far as pity. But you can't blame them."

"But this guy... this William and his wife... they *know* what they're doing... they know the consequences of their threats and their teachings... but they do it anyway. And you're right, that's scarier than the dark. It's scarier than any zombie."

"So you'll do it?" he asked, looking down at me.

I turned toward him and nodded up. "I will."

He touched my cheek and for a minute I think we both lost ourselves. The moment felt tender and real and it broke up the horror of everything we'd been through over the last forty-eight hours.

But reality had to set back in and I was the one who backed away. "Okay, so we need some kind of rope to get down to the awning."

I looked around for something that would serve the purpose and my gaze fell on the two beds.

"What about the sheets?"

Dave looked at the bed with worried eyes. "Um, didn't Mythbusters once do an episode about how you couldn't use sheets as a way out of prison?"

I laughed. "I don't remember if they busted it or not. But I guess we'll have to field test it again for them. There isn't anything else and I think the drop without any kind of way to slow it might get us hurt."

He shrugged, but I could see he was nervous. Have I mentioned Dave is a little afraid of heights? When my Mom came to visit and we took her to the Space Needle a year ago, he wouldn't look out the window. He just stood in the shop in the middle of the dome, pretending to check out postcards. So the fact that he'd recommended climbing out a window... well, it meant our situation was pretty bad.

"I'll go first," I promised as I started stripping the bed. "And catch you if you fall."

"Great," he laughed as he threw the pillows on the floor on the other side of the bed. "I'll remember you said that when I land on you."

CHAPTER 18

Show physical affection. Nothing says 'I love you' like bearing the entirety of your spouse's body weight.

Looks great," I said as I watched Dave finish securing our makeshift sheet ladder to the radiator.

He had braided the sheets from both beds together until they were a strong, cohesive rope and the knots he used on the radiator looked as powerful as any I'd ever seen. These were the times I was glad I had married a former Boy Scout. Those rope-tying skills had come in handy more than once during our relationship.

What? Everyone experiments. Don't judge.

Anyway, I pushed the window open as wide as I could and slung the rope out into the night. It swung gently in the breeze before it settled above the awning below.

"It doesn't quite reach," I said with a sigh. "But the drop is a lot less."

I looked back to find Dave staring at me, eyes wide. He was trying to control the fear, but I could see it was hitting him hard now that the time had come to actually go out a two-story window.

I patted his arm. "Hey, it's going to be fine. Look, I'll go first."

Dave tensed, but before he could argue I swung out over the edge of the window and held tightly to the sheet as I began to shimmy down.

Here's the thing if you ever decide to rappel out a window: wear gloves. By the time I reached the bottom of the sheet, my hands were raw and sore from the friction of the cotton fabric rubbing against them.

I was so ready to let go at that point that I really had to think hard about how I wanted to land so that I wouldn't just drop willy nilly. Luckily I hit the awning just right, with only the barest creak of the old metal, and stepped back to give my husband some room.

I looked up. Dave was still staring down at me from the window.

"It's okay," I called up, trying to make my voice soft and yet still let it carry to him. "It's not so bad."

That was a lie, of course. Dave was bigger than I was, so he was going to struggle with the pain of the descent as much, if not more than I had, thanks to his added body weight. But I didn't think it made much sense to tell him that when the height of the drop already made him nervous. So I merely gave him the thumbs up and held my breath.

"I can't do this, Sarah," he finally whispered down.

"Oh shit," I muttered to myself.

I knew he had issues with the height, but I hadn't even thought about the possibility that he might freeze. And I wasn't up there to help him, to push him.

"David," I said, my voice sharp to make sure he was paying attention. When he nodded, I continued, "You *can* do this, babe. Look at me."

His face was pale, but he focused on mine in the light above.

"You can do this," I repeated. "You *have* to do it for me."

To my surprise, that woke him up. He grabbed the sheet in both hands and swung out over the ledge. I could see him dragging in heaving breaths, but he started down toward me slowly.

The closer he came, the more I could see the agony on his face. Just like I had, he was struggling with the unexpected friction of the cotton on his palms. But unlike me, he didn't make it all the way to the bottom before he ground out a curse and then the sheet slipped from his hands with a whizzing sound and he fell.

He landed at a weird angle and then went down on his backside. At first I thought he was okay, but then he started rocking gently as he grabbed his leg and bit his lip so he wouldn't make too much noise and attract any zombies...or cult leaders...waiting around outside.

I dropped down on my knees next to him and grabbed his arm. I wanted to cry out as I watched his face constrict with pain, but I couldn't.

"Babe," I whispered just under my breath. "Oh, baby, are you okay?"

He shut his eyes hard and I watched him struggle to pull it back together, but then he nodded. "Yeah," he bit out. "I'm okay. Let's just get moving."

I had my doubts, but Dave wasn't waiting to decide our next move by committee. With a moan worthy of any brain-seeking zombie he dragged himself to the edge of the awning and looked down. It was about a seven-foot drop. Definitely doable, especially since we intended to dangle from the edge, but if he was already injured...

Well, we'll just say it added a new element to the idea. But I'll give him credit. He sucked it up, he manned it up and he hung over the side of the overhang. He drew in a deep breath and then he dropped.

I went over the side as fast as I could and let go, landing with a jarring hit on the ground, but I wasn't hurt. Dave, on the other hand, sat on the ground, holding his leg as silent tears streamed down his face.

"Shit," I whispered as I put my arm around him to help him to his feet. "It's bad, isn't it?"

He nodded silently. "Let's go, we just have to go."

I let him brace on me for support and we started in a limping run across the parking lot.

There are times in a marriage when one person has to give a little more for the other one. I knew this was my day and for once I didn't bitch about it.

As Dave bit his lip in agony at my side, I scanned the lot for a car that had keys in the ignition. Anything, any piece of shit would do. I no longer cared about satellite radio or bucket seats. I just wanted to get Dave into a car where he wouldn't have to put weight on his fucked up leg and get us as far away from here as I could.

We were about halfway across the parking lot when I heard a roar behind us. I looked over my shoulder while we continued to run and I was shocked to see that it wasn't zombies who made the sound.

From the door of the casino, the members of the cult were rushing out toward us, their wild charge led by William. His blond hair streamed out behind him and with the light behind him he actually did look like a messenger of God, sent to deal with sinners like us.

"Run, baby," I urged Dave. "Run!"

He limped as fast as he could, but I could feel him slowing down with every step as he fought the pain of his injury. I looked back again and the cult members had erased half the distance between us. They were carrying machetes and knives and one even had a sword.

They were going to butcher us when they caught us. And I was terrified by that prospect. I can admit that now, hell, I would have admitted it then. I could hardly breathe as I pictured all the awful things they would do before we died. It was worse, I think, because we had survived so many zombies only to probably get killed by a bunch of freaks who were twisting the Bible for their own purposes.

But just as they started to close the final distance, close enough that I could see William's bright eyes sparkle in the parking lot lights, a horde of zombies broke from the trees on the left side of the parking lot.

I almost came to a stop at the shock of seeing them attacking as a group. There were too many to count. Probably even more than there had been when we burned the car in the International District back in Seattle. They rolled from the trees in a gray, sludge-sprewing, limping wave, growling with hunger and pain.

I had never been so happy to see them before in my life. Their appearance distracted the cult and they turned toward the galloping horde to let out a war cry.

"Purge the unclean!" William bellowed and he charged toward them.

"Run!" Dave whispered. "Go, go, go!"

I shook off my surprise and started booking it across the parking lot again. One of the zombies broke toward us and caught up to us pretty easily since we were slowed down by Dave's injury. I pushed my husband behind me and did the thing you always see at some point in zombie movies.

I went all kung fu on his zombie ass.

I sucked at it, too. The thing they don't tell you in all the zombie movies is that zombies are a bit...squishy. If you think about it, it makes perfect sense. They are the living dead, after all, and their flesh is rotting away slowly but surely.

So when the first zombie reached us I did a straight kick into his abdomen. I expected him to fly backward a la *The Matrix*, but instead my foot sank into his flesh, almost like it was landing in really squishy quicksand.

The zombie and I stared at each other for a second, our twin expressions of confusion probably pretty comical. But then he bared his teeth and growled at me. Black sludge rolled down his chin and his red eyes glinted in the parking lot lights.

"Oh hell, no!" I grunted, then I pulled my leg away from his spongy stomach and instead did a big high kick across his chin.

That rocked him back and he staggered away into a parked car. His back hit the side mirror and to my shock it pierced his rotted skin and went straight through until it bulged out through his shirt, the mirror perfectly outlined though the plaid fabric.

"Ew," Dave and I both said together.

The zombie grunted and tried to pull away from the mirror, but he was stuck. I shook off my disgust and surprise. This was our opportunity! I grabbed Dave and we started running again. The zombie roared behind us and I glanced back to see a few more breaking away from the main group that was fighting the cult.

"Car, we need a car," I muttered. Without any other weapons, that was the only way out.

"There!" Dave said, his voice strained as he motioned a row over.

I hurried in the direction he'd indicated until I saw the car with the big wad of keys dangling from the ignition. It was sitting under a light and the keyring *was* fluorescent green, but I still patted Dave's shoulder as I threw the door open and shoved him into the passenger seat.

"Good eyes."

I hurried around the car, trying not to be entirely appalled by the vehicle. So Dave and I had owned a shitty car. Mid-90s-style sedan, no frills beyond a CD changer. It was rusty and loud and it smelled like cheese fries when we ran the heater in the winter.

But that car looked like a luxury model when compared to this. An early-80s-model boat, later Dave told me it was a Chevy Caprice, it was this awful shade of blue...at least where the cake of dirt and the red rusty spots were cleared a bit.

As I got in, I sort of thought that this was the kind of car the owner probably just left the keys in all the time. I mean, who would steal it?

I slammed the door shut and metal ground against metal with a grinding, crushing sound. But I'd done it just in time because not one but *three* zombies hit my side of the car at the same time. I let out a really girly scream as they clawed at the big car's windows, smearing them with blood and sludge as they drooled on the glass and tried to dig their way in.

My hands shook as I turned the key and the massive V8 engine roared to life. I pulled out of the parking space in reverse with my foot to the floor and swung the wheel, sending the zombies on my side of the car flying through the air. It was very satisfying to see them soaring across the parking lot, bouncing off cars and poles.

For a minute Dave and I looked at the scene around us. I had turned the car toward the battle being waged between the cult members and the zombies. We stared, silent, as the humans swung their blades, lopping off zombie heads just like we were watching a video game.

But occasionally the zombies got their points, too. A few clung to the necks of the living, biting and clawing at live flesh with the zeal of a rabid animal.

I craned my neck and found William in the fray. He was slashing at a group of zombie children, hacking them to bits with a joy that was a bit frightening. Then he turned toward our car lights and stared at us. His expression was angry and bitter. He scowled as he started across the parking lot toward us. I was about to throw the car into drive and get the fuck out of there when a zombie stood up on top of a van next to the "prophet."

With a growl, he jumped and landed squarely on top of William. They fell to the ground in a tangle of arms and legs and clawing fingers. The zombie dug his teeth into the preacher's flesh without hesitation. William's screams were faint through the glass and I shook my head. I guess God hadn't protected him after all.

"Look," Dave said.

He motioned toward the entrance to the casino.

Standing there, watching everything unfold, was Melissa Blackwell. She stared as the zombie devoured her husband, draining his life and damning him to walk the earth as the undead.

But before I could feel too sorry for her for what she was seeing, she turned around and went back into the casino, ushering the women and children who stood around her back inside.

"It looks like the Blackwell Truth Church has a new leader," Dave said with a shake of his head

I thought of Melissa and her sharp, intelligent eyes and strong grip on my arm earlier in the night.

"God help them," I murmured as I pulled around in a big circle and headed out into the dark night and all the uncertainty that faced us.

CHAPTER 19

Admit when you're wrong. It doesn't fix a busted leg,
of course, but it's a nice gesture nonetheless.

Under normal circumstances, the park we pulled into
near the airport probably would have been a very dangerous place. It wasn't well-lit for one thing. The light we'd
parked under barely flickered and two of the others were
burned out entirely.

Because of its proximity to the airport, it would normally be filled with jet noise all night and all day, which
meant the neighborhood wasn't exactly prime and ended
up attracting a bad element that led to a high crime rate.

But tonight there were no drug dealers to be contended
with, there was no one lurking in the shadows hoping to
take a car or a life... or at least no one who could actually
be blamed for their intentions. I was sure there were plenty
of zombies outside, but they didn't know any better.

Outside wasn't my problem, anyway. We had plenty to
deal with within the four doors of the car.

"Climb into the back if you can," I said softly as I
turned the engine off.

Dave flinched as he unbuckled his seatbelt. He turned sideways with a sucking sound of breath through his teeth and looked at the seat. Because the car was so low, it was a long seat but it wasn't very high. He shut his eyes briefly and then dragged himself over the top and into the wide backseat. He managed to bite back most of his sounds of pain and cursing, but there was no doubt his leg was in a bad way.

Once he had settled in, I slid to the passenger side of the vehicle and opened up the glove compartment. We had been able to take nothing with us in our escape, so all I could do was pray I'd find something of use.

The glove box matched the car in that it was big, old, and dirty, but there were some cheap cigarettes and a lighter right in the front of the pile. I pocketed the lighter for future use.

When I dug around further, I came up with a small bottle of whiskey, which I passed back to David without a word. Whether he used it for pain relief or we kept it to clean future wounds, it was a good find.

"Hey, look at this," Dave said from the back.

I turned in the seat to see that he was holding up a GPS unit. I shook my head in surprise. "With such a shitty car...who knew?"

He looked at it. It was so brand new that it still had the plastic seal over the display screen, but there wasn't any packaging with it.

"It was hidden under the seat, so it could be hot. Either way, it will come in handy if the satellites are still linked for the system."

I remained silent. The word *if* implied they might not be. If that was true it meant that in less than three days an outbreak that had started in Seattle had basically wiped out the United States and maybe the world.

The hugeness of that was overpowering. It rose up in my chest and stole my breath, but I had too much to do to freak out, so I put it from my mind and kept digging through the cavern of a glove box.

I pulled out papers and other junk until I got to the back of the compartment. My hand brushed something cold and metal and I smiled. Hidden behind everything was a small-caliber handgun and a half-full box of bullets.

"Lookie here," I said, holding them up with a grin as wide as any child on Christmas morning.

"That's great!" Dave sighed with relief. "At least we're not totally unarmed, though that thing isn't going to have much effect unless you get a clean headshot."

"There isn't much ammo, either," I conceded as I tossed the weapon on the seat beside him and climbed into the back. "But it's better than nothing. Now let me see your leg."

He hesitated before he lifted the injured leg into my lap. I rolled up his pants and sucked in my breath through my teeth with a hissing sound. Dave's calf area on his right leg was one big bruise, swollen and ugly.

"Damn," he murmured as he flopped his head back against the seat. "That looks even worse than it feels."

"It looks bad, but I'm not sure if it's broken," I said as I felt along the bone. He winced with every touch, but I didn't feel any obvious fracture. "It could just be a deep bone bruise."

He nodded. "I sure wish we had some ice to reduce the swelling." He motioned to the bottle of whiskey with a half-smile. "And for this."

I grinned at him, but I didn't really feel much happiness. "I wish we had a lot of things."

He shut his eyes. "So let's just assess here. We have one small-caliber handgun with what...maybe twenty shots?"

I nodded as I rested my head against the seat the same way he was. "And no other supplies of any consequence."

"Right." He looked down. "And my leg is jacked, broken or not."

"Plus it's dark and we can't get on the highway until we're able to see better in the morning for navigation. And there might be...strike that, there are *definitely* zombies around here whether they've noticed us yet or not."

I shivered. I was trying to keep my voice calm, but there was no softening the bald facts.

He was quiet for a long time. So long, in fact, that I started to think he'd fallen asleep or passed out from the pain. But finally he turned his head and looked at me.

"Sarah, I'm sorry I let you down."

I drew back at his voice and his words and stared at him. "What are you talking about? You didn't let me down. You've been awesome since this happened. And you saved my life more than once."

"And put it in danger," he said as he rubbed his chin where two days' worth of scruff was present.

"It isn't your fault that a zombie plague is upon us," I insisted.

He rolled his head on the seatback to look at me. "Maybe not, but tonight you didn't want to go to the casino. You had a million good reasons not to do it, but you did anyway because I was so insistent. If I had just listened to you in the parking lot instead of being obsessed with checking the place out then we'd still have the Escalade and our supplies and I wouldn't be hurt."

I shrugged. Yes, all those things were true, but I guess all of Dr. Kelly's lessons about marriage and partnership were beginning to sink in because I wasn't pissed about them. Six months ago, I would have reamed him for the mistakes we'd made today. Right now I was just happy we still had our heads and each other.

"You don't know if all that is true," I said. "Even if we'd done what I wanted and tried to find a house to hide in for the night, we still might have encountered totally crazy people or been swarmed by zombies or gotten injured and lost our stuff some other way."

"But what if—"

I interrupted him by covering his hand. "We can play 'what if' until morning, but it won't change a thing. We both made decisions, and a lot of them we made together. Remember what I said before... we're new at this. I guess we've learned something for the next time."

Dave laughed through his obvious pain. "No casinos."

I chuckled with him. "A valuable life lesson one way or another. I don't want to end up a granny zombie tugging a slot machine handle until the end of time."

His laughter faded. "But before the attack, Sarah—"

I shook my head. "No, what you said to me before we went into the casino was right, even if I didn't want to hear it. I think it's time to stop looking back and second-guessing and hating ourselves, not to mention stop punishing each other. From now on, let's agree to move forward."

I extended my hand to shake on the agreement and he hesitated for a minute before he grabbed my hand and shook. "Agreed."

He smiled and I had the craziest urge to just kiss him. Kiss him like we were kids in high school making out in the backseat of this crappy car in a park in the middle of nowhere. I leaned in and he did, too, but before our lips met he straightened up and looked out the front window.

"Wow," he murmured, "Zombie jogger."

I craned my neck to see what he was looking at. I couldn't help but giggle. A hugely fat zombie was creeping his way down the jogging path in front of the parking lot. He was dressed in a green velour tracksuit and had a lime headband straight out of eighty-five. Actually, it might have been purchased at the same time as our crappy car first rolled off the assembly line.

"Wow is right," I agreed as I leaned back slowly. "It looks like fashion was undead for that guy long before he was."

"You have to give him credit for having a workout, though," Dave said. "I mean, he's doing something."

I laughed and Dave smiled as he reached out and locked the door next to him. I did the same.

"Why don't you rest your head on my shoulder and try to sleep?" he asked as he slipped the handgun from my fingers. "We'll take turns keeping watch. Not that Zombie Jogger seems that interested."

I wanted to argue with him that he should try to rest since he was injured, but I kept my mouth shut. Whatever I said to him, however much he denied it, it was obvious that David felt guilty about the situation we were in. Maybe standing guard for a few hours would help him get over that. Plus, I was so tired I could hardly keep my eyes open. Since I'd be doing most, if not all the driving the next day, I had to rest.

So I put my head on his shoulder, snuggling down as his arm came around me and he held me. The seat was big and surprisingly comfortable so before long I was sleeping, but I won't tell you about my dreams. They were far too vivid and terrifying to share.

And when I woke up, the reality wasn't much better.

CHAPTER 20

Find creative ways to have fun together.
Looting is really underrated.

Dawn sent rays of sunshine flooding into our car and I stretched my back as I looked down at Dave's pale face.

"Well, we're alive," I said as I smiled at him in the hopes he would smile back. "That's step one."

He nodded, but I could see how much he was hurting. He hadn't been able to elevate his leg much last night and I doubted he'd gotten more than an hour or two of sleep. I mentally added getting painkillers and sleep aids to the running 'to do' list in my head.

"Yeah, thanks to your good shooting in the middle of the night."

I shrugged. Although the night had been surprisingly quiet, we had encountered a couple of zombie incidents. There were half a dozen or so bodies scattered outside the car as a testament to that fact. I was *definitely* becoming a better shot through all of this.

"Still, it was better than we thought," I offered.

He leaned forward in his seat. I reached back and

began to rub his back. He let out a sigh of contentment as he said, "Whoever would have believed that being attacked six times and having to kill things in the middle of the night would be better than we thought?"

"The world, she is a-changing," I muttered.

He nodded, his gaze distant at that thought. "Yeah. You know, I think we've got to find a sporting goods store and a grocery today before we get back on the road."

He shifted and I massaged harder even as I found the GPS on the seat next to us with my free hand.

"The grocery store has to have a pharmacy, too. We need supplies for your leg," I added as I turned it on. We both stared at the loading screen. There was a bar across the bottom that said, "Searching for link-up..."

Slowly a red-colored bar inched across the bar, filling it up as the system searched for communication from the wider universe. We waited, neither of us breathing, to find out if we were all alone in the world, or if it was still possible that someone was out there.

When the screen turned blue and it said, "Link-up found. Where do you want to go today?" I could have cried. It was a slender reed of hope, but it still existed.

I used the "Search Points of Interest" function and quickly accessed all the local sporting goods stores. I figured we'd need weapons before food and other supplies.

"The first listing is Bingo's Sporting Depot. It's less than a mile from here," I said.

"Sounds good," Dave replied.

I started to climb over to the front seat, but Dave caught my belt loop and pulled me back. "I can't do that again, it hurts too much. I'm taking my chances with the zombies and getting out."

"Let me come around and cover you, at least," I said.

I hurried to get out of the car and was greeted with a burst of cool morning air. There was a light, low fog all around that made the vacant parking lot and far-too-quiet park even more eerie. I made a quick scan for zombies, then rushed over to his side of the car and helped him step onto the asphalt. Gingerly he put his weight on his leg and we both breathed a sigh of relief when he was able to bear the strain.

"You may be right about the bone bruise," he said as we limped to the front seat and got him settled in.

I hoped that was true as I took the handgun and went around the back of the car. Last night it had been too dark to check for supplies, but since I was already out, I was going to go all the way. I checked in every direction probably a hundred times before I used the key to open the trunk and looked inside.

There was both a baseball bat and a tire iron inside and I grabbed them both in one hand. In addition there were some blankets and a first aid kit. I swept them all up and slammed the trunk shut.

The sound brought a rustle in the woods to my right and I spun to face it, holding my shaking handgun as a defense against the potential onslaught. There was shuffling and movement through the brush and trees and then a cat rushed from the darkness with a hiss.

I tensed, thinking of my conversation with David the first day this started. Was it possible this was a zombie cat? Just because we hadn't seen a lot of animals since this started didn't mean they weren't out there...waiting.

But the tabby simply sat down in the middle of the parking lot and began to clean her leg with long, luxurious licks. It was like nothing in her world had changed. From her bored demeanor, at least it seemed like she hadn't been chased by zombies for two days. Which probably meant animals were uninteresting to them. Whatever the horde wanted, they only found it in humans.

"Lucky you, kitty," I muttered as I let out a huge sigh of relief.

I climbed into the car and shut and locked the door. Dave took my additional supplies and the gun and we buckled in. He held the GPS as I pulled out of the lot and back onto surface streets.

The turn-by-turn directions kept us busy for a little bit. I had to navigate around cars and bodies strewn everywhere, so the "time to destination" increased rather than decreased as we puttered along, but finally we pulled into another huge parking lot in front of a sporting goods store. It wasn't one of the big box ones, but it would do as long as there were weapons to be found within.

"Maybe you should stay in the car," I suggested as I looked at the big building rising up ominously before me.

Dave turned toward me, the baseball bat gripped tight in his hands. "Are you nuts? There's no way I'm letting you do this alone. At the very least, I'll push the cart so you can have your hands free."

I stared at him. He could stand and walk slowly, but in a zombie attack I was terrified he wouldn't react in time. What if I couldn't help him?

But I could see from the firm set of his jaw and the determination in his eyes that this subject wasn't open for debate. And in all honesty, I would have acted the same way if the situation was reversed.

With a sigh, I motioned for him to open his door.

We crossed the parking lot slowly, taking our time both to accommodate Dave's injury and to keep an eye out for any infected who were lurking around. I actually saw a few on the outskirts of the lot, but they didn't seem to be aware of us as they lurched and moved around like confused dogs or lost children.

The doors to Bingo's Sporting Depot were automatic, but someone had turned off that function at some point, so I had to push the heavy glass and metal weight apart, wedge myself in, and then shove with my back to get us inside the store and out of the dangerously open area of the parking lot.

Once we were inside, I was overwhelmed by sensory overload. It wasn't that the place was a big store, but there was a lot of inventory. Enough that the areas with racks and fixtures were almost too tight to walk in.

"I don't like this," I whispered. "We won't be able to see or move much if we get off the main walkways."

Dave nodded and looked around above at the brightly colored signs hanging from the ceiling that labeled where all the different equipment was located. There were golf areas, team sports, stuff to boat and fish...but tucked in the back, in a special area was a sign that read, HUNTING AND GUN SUPPLIES.

We smiled at each other as we grabbed a cart from the front of the store and made our way to the back. As we passed by racks of clothing, I pulled off a few shirts for me and for David, as well as a new pair of hiking boots, the *really* expensive kind that I never would have paid for before the attack.

To be fair, my Keds *were* soaked with blood and I was

going to need something heavier duty if we encountered more roadblocks on our way to Longview.

Finally we reached the back corner of the shop and entered an area that was partly enclosed, sort of like a shop within a shop. Also known as Mecca. Behind the counter were racks of shotguns and rifles and in the glass case there were handguns. It all seemed to glow beautifully in the fluorescent lights and we stared at it for a long time with matching dopey grins on our faces.

"I'll get ammo," Dave finally offered before he limped off toward the shelves, using the cart as a walker.

As he did so, I looked at our weaponry options. Shotguns had proven themselves more than useful already, but in closer quarters I thought a 9mm handgun would be helpful, too. I laid a few shotguns on the counter and then dropped down to open the lower cabinet with the handguns. Just as I feared, the rack was locked. I sighed as I grabbed for one of the shotguns and bashed open the glass with the butt of it.

Immediately an alarm began to squeal in the background. I winced as I sent a look toward David.

"Sorry," I mouthed.

He shrugged as he wheeled the cart toward me and loaded up the weapons I'd already set out.

"You know, William may have been right about one thing," he mused as gun after gun went into the cart.

I tilted my head with a frown as I handed him another shotgun. "Zombies: scourge of God to cleanse the world?" I asked.

He flashed me a quick grin. "Well, *that* remains to be seen. But I mean he might have been right about loud sounds like the blast of a gun bringing zombies to investigate. We might want to get some sharp and blunt weapons for close-quarter fights just in case. Save the guns for just clearing the highway."

I shrugged. "That boat of a car certainly has enough space for it. Why not?"

He glanced around. "We haven't seen any activity here, human or infected. Do you want to split up?"

I tensed. We hadn't done that since the outbreak started. I guess my face must have showed my feelings because he reached out and grabbed my hands.

"Just to save time, Sarah. We still need to hit a grocery and then get on the road."

Of course, his logic made perfect sense so I nodded. "You take the cart."

He smiled as he moved off in one direction through the store. I headed in the other, checking through the aisles as I went.

In the golf section I got a big, heavy driver and tucked it under my arm. Then a second baseball bat from the sport section. The one David had at present was made from ultra-light aluminum, but this one was solid wood. When I tapped it against my palm it made a satisfying thud that I could almost imagine hearing when dealing with a zombie's rotting head.

I moved back toward the front of the store. At the cash registers there was a soda cooler and some power bars and other snacks. I grabbed some bags and loaded up with a bunch of each. Just as I was finishing up, I heard a sound behind me. I turned, expecting to find Dave waiting for me with our cart.

There was a person behind me, but I'm afraid it wasn't my husband. To my surprise, a pale-faced girl zombie stood in front of me. She was wearing a Bingo's nametag that read CINDY. Or at least it would have if there wasn't blood splattered across most of it.

Oh yeah, and she was missing an arm.

"Shit!" I yelped, dropping everything in my arms as she lunged toward me with a grunt and a whine.

She caught me before I could get any one of my many weapons in hand and we staggered toward the cash register together. I fell across the countertop, my hip hitting the edge with what I knew was bruising force.

Cindy the Zombie gnashed her teeth at me and I kicked upward, hitting her squarely between the legs. Unfortunately, her being a girl and all, the action didn't faze her. She only tilted her head at me and growled louder.

"David!" I screamed as I shoved her back with all my might, which wasn't much from the odd angle I was lying at.

Luckily for me though, because she didn't have an arm, she was off-balance already and she fell off of me and slid across the linoleum floor with a groan of whatever was the emotionless version of disappointment. But she moved right back for me, crawling across the floor with her jaws snapping.

In the distance, I saw Dave maneuvering his cart toward me. He had to lean on it for support, but he was making pretty good time considering his bum leg. Still, he wasn't going to make it before the girl hit me again, so I bolted, jumping behind the cashier desk like it was a bunker in a World War II simulation game.

The zombie lunged behind me and ended up lying across the counter making little biting faces at me as she pushed herself up on her tiptoes and slid as close as she could in my direction.

I don't know what came over me, really. I guess it was instinct... or maybe the faint, but wholly unpleasant memory of my days working in retail when I wished I could kill snotty holiday shoppers like I now killed zombies. Either way, I hit the cash out button on the old cash register and the drawer flew open.

It smacked Zombie Cindy right in the temple, breaking her rotting flesh and sending a light spray of tissue and blood across the countertop. She roared her pain as she glanced up at me with annoyance on her face.

Yup, that was just as satisfying as I'd always thought it would be during all those years ringing up ill-tempered shoppers.

I didn't wait for her to recover from the blow. There was a fixture rod sitting behind the counter and I grabbed the light metal with both hands.

"Sorry, Cindy," I muttered as I raised it over my head. "This is the cash-only lane. We don't accept gnashing teeth as credit."

I slammed the fixture down, smacking the confused and angry zombie right at the base of her skull. She whimpered, though her movements slowed and I smashed it down a few more times until she twitched and then lay still.

Just as I finished, Dave got to the front of the store. He slowed his pace as I dropped the bloody rod and came out from behind the counter. I wiped my hands off on my shirt and then looked down at myself.

Once again, I was covered in blood and brains and all kinds of disgusting mung that I don't even want to talk about. With a grunt, I peeled off my t-shirt and turned it inside out to wipe off my body as best I could.

Grabbing for the nearest rack, I replaced it with a new "Just Do It" t-shirt from the Nike rack and then gathered all the items I had been forced to drop in the struggle. Oddly, I was mostly irritated that the cold sodas were probably all shaken up now and we'd have to be careful opening them.

Dave remained silent the entire time, just watching me as I put myself back together.

"Sarah, are you okay?" he finally asked, his tone wary.

Of course it's not every day you get to watch your spouse beat the shit out of a zombie. Well, except by then I guess it was.

I shrugged as I stepped over the dead zombie and headed for the door.

"I think Dr. Kelly was right after all," I said as I dropped the items I'd grabbed into his cart and wedged the double doors open again. "You don't have to spend money to have a good time together. Look how much fun we had today and we haven't spent a dime."

Dave shook his head. "Well, technically, I think that's because we're looting."

"Potato/Potahto," I laughed as we moved into the parking lot. "Whatever it is, it's free."

CHAPTER 21

Do special things for each other.
Antibiotics are the gift that keeps giving.

The grocery store just across the way from Bingo's had a pharmacy, so we drove over what would have once been a main thoroughfare you never would have dared to cross without a light. But I can tell you what: There was going to be no splitting up this time as we entered the building.

It wasn't one of the big chain stores with their nice aisles and fancy name brand products. It had an old, "neighborhood store" feel to it that was kind of nice.

Unfortunately, it also meant it had been pretty well cleaned out when the infection started to break. The aisles were strewn with leftover food that had been cleared from the shelves in the melee of three days before. But I wasn't as worried about food, honestly. We had more pressing matters to deal with.

"There's the pharmacy," I said as I motioned toward the back of the store. Dave pushed a cart again as we made our way toward the glass-encased area in the back.

At first I felt pretty good about where we were. It was quiet, the lights and refrigerators were still running, and aside from the messy state of the food aisles, there wasn't much sign of infestation.

That was, at least, until the swinging doors in the back opened and from them fell a group of five zombies. Three of them were dressed in store uniforms and two had clearly once been customers. One was a middle-aged woman with curlers still in her hair; another was dressed up like she'd been on her way to or home from an office job, probably in some kind of management position if her tailored appearance (aside from the greyness and blood and sludge drooling, of course) was any indication.

"Man," I whined as I hopped behind the pharmacy counter and drew out a shotgun. "We just can't catch a break."

I fired the first shot as they started to move toward us and dropped Middle Management Zombie. The spray of the pellets caught Curler Zombie, too, and she flinched as her arm flopped from the impact. Dave braced himself on the end cap of a shelf and fired two shots in rapid succession, making quick work of the Curler Zombie I had winged and one of the store workers. I finished off the other two and reloaded before I turned into the back of the pharmacy.

"I'll just be a minute," I promised and hoped I'd be right.

There were short aisles behind the glass with drugs that seemed to be organized by what they treated so I started from the front and moved back.

I was disappointed that most of the painkillers had already been wiped out when the looting started a couple of days before. I guess the druggies and the people who were afraid of facing what was happening had taken advantage. But there were still some anti-inflammatories left behind so I grabbed those while Dave cleared out the supply of Tylenol on the other side of the glass. It would be better than nothing in a pinch.

I turned down the final aisle and came to a sudden stop. There on the floor were two bodies that I approached with caution. I nudged the first one with my foot, but it didn't move. It was actually a dead person, not a zombie.

I tilted my head to look closer. She was a woman, probably about my age, with a white lab coat and her hair pulled back in a bun. Her nametag said ANGELICA. She almost looked like she was just taking a rest, except that all around her mouth was a foamy substance and clutched in her hand was a big bottle of the powerful painkiller Oxycontin.

She must have been trapped back here when the zombies came in. Behind the glass she would have been able to see everything play out. And I guess she'd figured it was better not to let it happen to her.

With a sigh, I moved to the next body. But as I neared it, it jolted and I braced myself for a zombie encounter as it flipped over to face me. This one was the male pharmacist, probably a good twenty years older than the other girl. He had thinning grey hair that matched his skin and a friendly face, even though it was now twisted with a desire to crush me and eat my bones.

I drew back with a gasp I couldn't have kept to myself no matter how much you paid me. While the younger woman had taken her own life, it seemed like this man had decided to fight. And he'd lost because he was missing his legs. He scooted toward me on his belly, hissing and biting the air as he dragged himself through the pool of his own blood and tissue.

My empty stomach turned. I hoped he had already been a zombie when he sustained those injuries. The infected didn't seem to feel pain the way we did. It obviously irritated them when they were hurt, but they could soldier on without an arm or a leg.

"Sorry, buddy," I murmured as I swung my shotgun butt and smashed the side of his head in. He sighed, almost in relief, as his red pupils faded to lifeless black.

"What's up back there?" Dave asked and I realized I'd been standing out of his line of sight for a long time.

I grabbed a few more items, including some instant ice packs, and came out to where he could see me.

"Nothing," I said as I vaulted over the counter. I kept trying to put the image of the legless creature out of my mind. "Just taking care of an issue and I figured it didn't require wasting shells."

"Okay," Dave responded slowly, watching me closely as he took the armfuls of items I'd picked up and put them into the cart.

"Is that it?" I asked with false brightness as I looked around us.

He nodded. "I grabbed more nonperishables from the aisles close by. There's not much left here, I don't think, but if you want to we could look for more."

I stared at our cart, half full of items. I didn't want to stay here. I didn't want to have to keep finding zombies and bodies and fight. I was tired and I just wanted it all to stop. Of course, I knew it wasn't possible, but I shook my head like maybe it could be if we just left the store.

"If we make it to Longview tonight we can figure out the supply situation there," I said. "Knowing your sister, she has a bunker filled with homemade preserves that we can survive in for years."

Dave smiled. "See, she *could* come in handy."

I laughed softly. "At last. And even if we don't get there tonight, we'll have to stop somewhere anyway. Maybe we'll find someplace that hasn't been touched by..."

I trailed off and waved my hand at the carnage all around us.

He didn't answer, not that I blamed him. At this point, and after everything we'd seen and heard and done, I think we were pretty well aware that this terror had spread like crazy and there wasn't much of a safe place anymore, especially in the Western part of the United States. But I think we were still reluctant to say it out loud. Like it would jinx us or something if we admitted it.

"Then let's get back on the highway," he said, but his voice had the same ring of false cheer that mine had had earlier.

I led the way with him pushing the cart behind me. Just as we reached the front registers, another one of the infected popped up from behind the bigger "guest ser-vices" desk at the front. Without missing a beat, David shot him and he fell back down as if he'd never even existed.

Out in the parking lot, we loaded up the car as fast as we could, rearranging things so that we could get to them without being forced to stop.

As I pulled out, Dave put an ice pack on his leg and downed four Tylenol and a couple of the anti-inflammatories, then he handed me the carton of orange juice he'd found in a front cooler on our way out of the store.

While we maneuvered through the streets toward the highway with the GPS jabbering in our ears about which turn to take, we had a breakfast of stale muffins, juice, and ultra-fizzy Diet Coke (hey, I need my morning caffeine).

And as we rolled back up onto the congested road, I don't know what he was thinking, but the mantra that kept running through my head was, "Here we go again."

CHAPTER 22

Men are from Mars....Zombies are from Hell.

About fifteen miles past Sea-Tac airport the highway slowly...and rather eerily cleared up. It was as if this was as far as anyone had managed to make it and now we were pioneers on the next leg of our journey.

As we stopped having to weave within traffic, I glanced at Dave. His mouth was a thin line that expressed his worry as well as my own thoughts did.

"We're close to Tacoma," he murmured.

I nodded. "There should still be tons of traffic."

Honestly, the roads around here were pretty much bad until you got past Olympia and entered into full-blown rolling hills of bucolic farm country.

He reached out and turned on the old car's radio. I should also mention it had an eight track. Yes, that's how awesome our car was. But the radio was currently on FM stations and Dave turned the dial back and forth, looking for any kind of signal. Nothingness greeted us.

My heart was pounding. This was the first time our

attempts at finding a station had failed. Did that mean they were all gone?

"Try AM," I whispered, my voice shaking.

Without a word, he pressed the button that switched the feed and started rolling through AM stations.

Empty air and static were all we found. He wound the dial all the way to the bottom, then back to the top.

"Wait," I cried, "Was that a voice?"

He turned back just a little and sure enough, faint and clouded by static, was the voice of a young woman.

"The government might try to shut us up, but they can't shut us down," she said, her voice shaky and exhausted. "We *will* talk about the spread of the infection. We *will* tell you what we're seeing whether they like it or not."

I stiffened. "Did she just say the government was trying to shut her up?"

I guess I was still pretty innocent at that point. I figured that the government, *our* government, would be trying to figure out a way to share information, to save people who were left, not hush this disaster up.

"I'd guess it's a way to quell panic," Dave offered as he jacked the volume up so we could hear better over the bad reception.

"Here in..."

Her voice cut out so I couldn't hear where she was broadcasting from. It couldn't be far, though, the signal wasn't strong enough.

"...there are far more infected now than survivors. We have seen government tanks rolling through the streets. They've knocked down buildings without even checking for survivors inside. They have bombed city blocks and shot people who tried to flag them down for help."

My hand came up to cover my mouth, so it was good we were on open road now.

"Christ," I breathed.

"They're shutting down the power in…"

Again her voice crackled and I was frustrated in my attempts to figure out where she was.

"…and we're now running on a generator until it runs out of power…or *they* find us. The zombies or the soldiers. Please, spread the word. Don't listen to the reports that the outbreak is over and being contained. It isn't. And if you're hearing this from outside Portland…please find a way to tell others. Before it's too late."

The voice died and Dave began to roll the dial frantically as he tried to find her again, but she was gone.

"Portland," I breathed. "*Portland*? She had to be in Oregon."

He nodded as he snapped the radio off with a sigh of frustration. "She has to be. It's the only Portland close enough to have a signal. With a big enough transistor and enough power, she could reach us. Especially with all the other station chatter gone."

He rested his head back on the seat and his fists clenched at his sides. Tears stung my eyes and I had to focus to stay on the road. For the first time since all this began, I was really ready to lose it.

Longview was just at the Washington/Oregon border. About an hour north of Portland.

I sucked in a breath. "But if it's in Portland…if it's so bad in Portland that they're fire bombing the city, that means it's spread *past* Longview."

He nodded.

"It wouldn't skip a town, David," I sobbed. "Lisa was right. There isn't a Longview left."

"Pull over," he said softly.

"I can't, I have to—"

He touched my arm, his fingers gentle and soothing. "Pull over."

Slowly, I made it to the side of the road, putting the passenger wheels right on the shoulder, not that there was anyone else out there to hit me. Apparently the world that we knew of was officially gone.

I rested my head on the steering wheel and sobbed. Dave slid across the seat and put his arm around me. We sat like that for probably twenty minutes as I tried to pull it together without much success. But finally I guess I ran out of tears.

I sat up, wiping my nose on the bottom of my formerly clean t-shirt. "Okay, I'm sorry. I shouldn't have freaked out like that."

"Don't be sorry," he said, pushing some hair off my face. "If anyone deserves a breakdown it's us."

"But *we* didn't break down," I hiccupped. "I did."

"Well, I owe you one, then," he said as he slid back into place. We sat in silence for a while longer as I hiccupped out the last of my sobs and he was lost in thought.

Finally, he said, "Look, maybe we shouldn't go to Longview after all."

I jerked in my seat to face him. "What?"

He shrugged. "We know this infection or outbreak or whatever you want to call it has gone south, at least to Portland, maybe beyond. But we don't know for sure about east. Maybe even north toward Canada."

"So you think they stopped it at the border?" I asked incredulously.

He looked at me. "They won't even let us bring fireworks across. They're tough."

I stared at him for a long moment and then I couldn't help but laugh at the idea of the border patrol asking a zombie what his purpose was in going to Canada today.

Before I could answer, though, a handful of zombies started out of the wooded area on the side of the highway. I looked at them, lurching and sprewing. They had ruined our lives, they had killed our friends.

And in that moment, I didn't feel sorry for them anymore. I *hated* them.

I gunned the car as I threw it in gear and roared toward them.

"Fuck you, fuckers!" I screamed as I slammed into the first one.

He cartwheeled pretty comically over the car's wide hood, his jaws snapping at us even as he flipped upside down. The car thumped as I hit the second one, pulling her under my wheels with a thud and then a second thud when my back tires ran over her.

"What are you doing?" Dave asked as he scrambled for his seatbelt and held on to the door for dear life.

"Remember Dr. Kelly's scream therapy?" I asked.

"Yelling out our anger and purging it? You thought that was bullshit!" Dave protested.

"It was!" I agreed. "But Kill Therapy isn't. Tell those zombies what you think!"

He stared at me and then his gaze shifted to the male zombie in the jeans and t-shirt who was hurtling toward us up the side of the highway.

"Go to hell, you jackoff!" he said.

"No, yell it!" I said as we slammed into him. He

landed up on our hood, his face smooshed against the glass like a kid on a shop window.

"Fuck YOU!" Dave bellowed before he reached over to my side and turned on the windshield wipers. They smacked the zombie's face and he growled before I spun the wheel and sent him flying off the hood to land on his head in the ditch.

With all the zombies taken care of, I stopped the car again and faced Dave. "We aren't going east and we aren't going north. We're going to Longview to find your sister. I may hate that bitch, but if she isn't a zombie then she belongs with us. No man... er, woman left behind, you got that, soldier?"

Dave stared at me. "Okay. Okay! So let's go to Longview."

"Let's go to mother-fucking Longview."

CHAPTER 23

Pick the right time to broach a delicate subject.
Sometimes the hillbilly will give you the
answers in his own time.

The moment we pulled off the highway toward Longview four excruciating hours later, it was obvious that the place was a ghost town. The steel and chemical plants, which normally sent steam and smoke billowing up into smelly plumes across the sky, were both eerily silent and still. We turned at the bottom of the off ramp and headed toward the main street of town.

Longview was a classic small Washington state town. Surrounded by wonderful outdoor beauty, the thirty-five thousand residents mostly made their livings at the factories or in the service of those who did. Economic times had been tough in the last few years, but the town had pulled together. They took care of their own.

They had a traditional main street with little shops and restaurants, which was one of the only reasons I actually liked coming here when David dragged me down to visit his sister. There was always something new to see or some new craftsperson to speak to in those stores.

Not that we had a choice but to come here. Gina refused to come to Seattle. She said she was "afraid" of the traffic and of being raped. No amount of discussion on the matter would change her mind. When she pictured the city...any city, she seemed to picture bumper-to-bumper traffic and rape...quite possibly together.

Not that it mattered now, I guess. I mean, if the girl on the pirated radio station was right and they were fire-bombing Portland to end the plague, then they were probably doing the same behind us in Seattle.

"Wow," Dave breathed, dragging me from my thoughts as I looked down Main Street.

The charming shops I'd liked so much had obviously seen some action from the infected...or looters...or both. Almost every window was shattered, some of the shards remaining in the windows as a bloody testament to a zombie war it didn't seem like we could win.

We drove along the streets. A burned-out husk of a classic car was parked half on the sidewalk, still smoldering.

"I wonder if that means it was fair time?" David asked.

Every year in early August, the town had a big fair. Normally we came down for it, but this year with the problems in our marriage and our financial difficulties, I hadn't kept track of when the big event was. But the classic car was a good indication. They always did a parade, followed by a classic car show to kick off the event.

"There are the signs," I said, motioning to the big Cowlitz County Fair signs that pointed toward the Expo Center. "Want to check it out?"

Dave didn't answer, he was too busy looking at the bodies that were strewn across the sidewalk in the distance. I'm sure he was thinking about his sister, Gina. She never missed a parade, so she would have been here when all hell broke loose.

I was thinking about her, too, but in a way I wanted to put off looking for her. The longer we waited, the longer it was going to be before we found out she was a zombie or dead. Seeing the upheaval around us, I feared those were her only two options.

I followed the signs to the big, open area near the Expo Center. We were still a short distance away when I saw the Ferris Wheel all set up and ready for kids.

It was running.

"What the hell?" I said, looking up at the slowly spinning wheel. It was an eerie sight with the rest of the town all but deserted.

Dave swallowed. "It must have been running when the town was attacked."

"Do you think there are people up there?" I whispered.

"Ones who were stuck on the ride, you mean?" Dave asked, his eyes getting wide. "I hadn't thought about it, but maybe we should check."

I nodded as I pulled the car to a stop in the middle of the street. I grabbed a tire iron from the back, he took the baseball bat and we each had a shotgun as we got out of the car. I locked it behind us and Dave laughed.

"Worried about the hoodlums, eh?" he asked.

I couldn't help but smile. "Hey, nothing good ever happens at a zombie carnival. Recent zombie movies have taught us that."

"So true," he said with a laugh. "And I guess my sister would approve of your prudence anyway."

His smile fell at that.

There wasn't any opportunity for comfort, though. He limped off ahead of me. I watched him as I trailed behind him. He was moving better now that he was regularly taking some over-the-counter painkillers and the prescription anti-inflammatories. I just hoped once we got to Gina's, we'd be able to better brace his leg up and get him whole again.

We passed through the fair gate and the empty ticket booth beside it. There was blood streaked on the brightly painted wood and sludge that had dried to a sticky, disgusting black.

"Activity," I said, not explaining myself further. I didn't have to. By this time, Dave just glanced at the evidence and grunted an acknowledgment by lifting his gun a little higher.

The happy, comforting smells of batter and hot dogs and cotton candy still wafted through the air, although they were mingled with the scent of smoke and blood now. It was an incongruous combination that was somehow becoming commonplace. Heaven with Hell. Life with death.

We headed through the different stalls that had been set up for food and crafts on the way toward the ride area. In the distance I heard the growling and moaning of zombies, but I didn't see any...yet.

The carnival area had the usual array of silly games for kids, complete with cheaply made, huge stuffed animals made by the labor of little children in far away factories, no doubt. I wondered if the outbreak would spread to them in time. Or if it already had.

I was so lost in my musings that I didn't see the zombie until he stood up at the "Balloon Pop" booth and started staggering over the low counter toward me. He was dressed in some hokey carnival caller outfit, complete with red striped shirt and a hat with a name tag pinned to it. HANK.

"You going to get that?" Dave asked from my left, his tone calm and bored. One zombie wasn't worth getting worked up about anymore, I guess.

I nodded as I raised my shotgun and was about to fire off a kill shot when an arrow whizzed past and hit Zombie Hank square in the forehead. The redness went out of his eyes immediately and he fell forward, landing right on his face in the dirt.

I spun around and so did Dave. A man in a dingy white tank top and jean shorts with cowboy boots came running up out of the mass of booths.

"Woohoo!" he shouted as he spit a disgusting plug of tobacco right at my feet. "Did you see that shot, girlie?"

"Sure did, much obliged," I managed to say as I stared. Yup, this was straight out of a zombie movie now. Hillbilly saves couple. But would it turn into *Deliverance*?

Dave limped forward with a look of relief and shock on his face. "Conrad?"

I blinked as I put a name to the familiar and yet wacky face before us.

Conrad Hanvers was Gina's neighbor up the road. He looked to be about fifty, but Gina said that was just from some hard living and that he was closer to thirty-five.

He was a nice guy when you looked past the crazy blond mullet, the farmer's tan, and the tobacco chewing. He had once helped us change a tire when we got a flat up here years ago and always came over to shovel Gina's drive when it snowed in the winter.

"Why if it ain't Davy Boy and Miss Sarah," Conrad said with a laugh. "Did you all come down here for the fair?"

I stared at him for almost a full minute before I looked at Dave. I hoped *he* would come up with something to say because I was speechless at this point.

"Uh," he started with an awkward shuffle of his feet. "No, Conrad, we didn't. We got chased out of Seattle by the, uh . . . well, the . . ."

He motioned to the zombie Conrad had just hit between the eyes. Conrad looked down at the dead man with a whistle.

"So the television was right, eh? So the whole world's gone to hell in a handbasket after all."

"I'm afraid so," I said, finally finding my voice somehow. "The whole city was overrun in a matter of about twenty-four hours. By the time we got out, I doubt there were many survivors left."

Conrad blinked. "Well, I'll be suckered. Those city slickers didn't put up much of a fight, did they?"

I shrugged, a little annoyed by the implication that we hadn't even bothered to try up north. I mean, this was a zombie invasion, something out of movies and nightmares. This wasn't something you just knew what to do when faced with it.

"I can see it made it down here, as well," Dave said, his voice tense enough that I could tell he was as irritated by the implication as I was.

Conrad looked around with a deep sigh. "Yes, yes. It all started about a day and a half ago. Some crazy mowed right through the fair day parade up Main Street in one of them classic cars. We thought he was a drunk, but when he got out, he started trying to *eat* people. It was the darndest thing. Aw, it took folks a while to sort it all out, but now we're getting the hang of it."

"The hang of it," David repeated blankly.

Conrad nodded. "Yup. We plug those poor bastards in the brains and take them to the burning pile over yonder."

He motioned off beyond the fairgrounds. In the distance I saw a faint line of black smoke curling up into the sky. I shivered at the thought that it was a big crematory.

"We even got patrols running twenty-four-seven now," Conrad finished with a shrug. "So I think we'll be okay."

After the last few days, I wasn't so sure about that, but at present I was just too exhausted to argue the point.

"We saw the Ferris Wheel running, that's why we came in here," I said, motioning toward the slowly turning ride in the distance. "No one is trapped on it, are they?"

Conrad looked over his shoulder toward the ride, but then he seemed to get distracted by something else he saw.

"Aw, no." He shrugged and then leaned his head to the side. "Hang on, darlin'."

He pulled an arrow from the Wal-Mart brand arrow holster attached to his hip. He set it into the bow and fired off a shot. In the distance I heard a thump and then a sickly groan before silence again.

"Hot damn, I'm on a roll!" Conrad said as he turned back. "Now what were we talking about?"

I looked at Dave. How could this guy be so...jubilant? His town was being overrun by monsters!

"Um, the rides," I said. "If there were people trapped on the rides."

Conrad pulled a can of chaw from his back pocket. "That's right. No worries, we got all the living people off. Some of the sick ones were still riding last I checked."

I looked up. Now that we were closer I could see there were people on the spinning chairs, lurching softly as the ride turned. I wondered what, if anything, the zombies thought of that.

"So how many did you lose?" I asked. "Before you 'got it under control'?"

Conrad shut his eyes, like he was doing complicated math in his head. "Well, all told I guess about seven or eight thousand."

I staggered back. "That's a quarter of the town."

He nodded and the joviality he had been expressing faded somewhat. He might talk a good game, but the horror of losing friends and neighbors wasn't lost on him.

"But now that we know what to do, I doubt that number will go up much," he said softly, almost like he was trying to convince himself.

Dave sidled closer, his face pale. "What about Gina, Conrad? Did you lose Gina?"

The other man turned on him. "Aw, hell, Gina. I should have told you right from the start. I swear sometimes I don't have the sense of a goat!"

"What about Gina?" Dave pressed, his teeth clenched.

"She's okay," Conrad hurried to say. "She was at the parade and nearly got herself killed by the first wave of those crazy bastards. But I helped her get to her truck and back toward home. I checked on her just this morning and she's just fine. Waiting it out just like everybody else."

Dave wobbled just a little and I caught his arm to steady him. "Thank God," he muttered.

"You all going to go down and see her?" Conrad asked.

I nodded, my own relief welling up in me. No, I wasn't Gina's biggest fan, but I didn't want the woman dead...or undead by any means! Especially since I knew how much Dave cared about her.

"Yeah, we're going that way now," Dave said, motioning me to leave the fair and head for the car.

"I'll come and check on you all later," Conrad said with a lopsided grin.

We waved goodbye and headed back out to the car. As we got in, Dave flopped his head back on the seat and sighed. "I can't believe they lost so much of the town."

I nodded, trying not to think of all those men and women and children who we had seen at the fair over the years. It was too awful to think about the infected flooding into the parade and attacking them, turning them against their own families and friends within moments.

I shivered as I pushed the thought from my head. I smiled at him.

"The good news is that Gina is okay. So what do you say we head on out her way and show her that her baby brother is alive and well."

CHAPTER 24

Cultivate a good relationship with your spouse's family. You never know when you might need shelter from a zombie storm.

Gina lived out in a little three-bedroom rambler just outside of town which was situated on about three acres of pristine land that she rented out to farmers for their crops.

She had gotten it in a divorce settlement with her high school boyfriend-turned-husband a few years back, along with pretty much everything else the poor guy ever had. I think he'd had to move back in with his parents by the time she was through with him. I'd always felt bad for him, really.

I guess I was the only one.

By the time we reached the house, the afternoon was getting long and the sun was starting to set. As we got out, I looked around for any signs of the infected, but in this secluded place there weren't any, or they were just too hidden to see. The house was intact with no broken windows or obvious blood or sludge on the grass, walls or door.

"Looks okay," Dave said with a relieved sigh, but the tension didn't leave his shoulders. I guessed it wouldn't until we'd seen Gina for ourselves.

I nodded as we went up to the door. I knocked and then stepped back. It was a good thing I did because the inside door flew open and the quiet afternoon was shattered by the explosive shot of a shotgun. The glass storm door shattered and Dave and I dove for cover in opposite directions to avoid the spray of pellets.

"Shit, Gina!" Dave bellowed as he rolled behind a planter on the messy porch. "It's us. Christ!"

Slowly a dark head came into view in the broken door. Gina stood there, gun in hand, and she looked at us like she didn't even recognize us.

"David?" she finally whispered.

"It's *us*." He nodded from behind the plant. "Put the gun down, Gina."

She lowered the shotgun and pushed the storm door open. Glass tinkled onto the porch as she did so.

"Is that really you?" she asked as she came out into the sunlight.

He got up slowly and so did I behind her. It took him longer because of his injury and his limp was more pronounced again as he moved toward her. Fuck, I hoped he hadn't hurt his leg any more than it already was.

"It's really us," he said as he put his arms around her.

She held him tight for a minute and my throat thickened at their reunion. All my bad thoughts about Gina faded.

Until she backed up and talked. "You're too skinny. Doesn't *she* feed you?"

I cleared my throat and arched a brow as the two turned

toward me. Gina's face fell before she pulled it together. I guess she must have hoped that Dave had finally had enough of me and abandoned me to the attacking horde.

"*She* feeds him three times a day at least," I said, forcing a smile. "And he's actually capable of feeding himself, too. Hi, Gina."

My sister-in-law smiled, but like me I could see it wasn't any more real than my own. Yeah, we'd never really seen eye to eye.

"Sarah," she said, stepping toward me for a brief hug that barely involved any pressure at all. "I'm so glad you're both here."

I looked at the destroyed glass door. "Me too."

She shrugged at my expression. "What else could I do? I didn't recognize the car and I didn't see you guys on the porch."

I waited for her to apologize for almost putting a spray of pellets in my body, not to mention her baby brother's, but she didn't. Instead she turned toward the house and motioned us in behind her.

"Come inside."

We entered the house and I stared around in surprise. Unlike me, Gina is totally a Martha Stewart. She's tidy, she makes things from scratch for holiday gifts that always turn out perfectly and even more to decorate her house. Her place, although small, is a bit of a showplace. The one time she came to our apartment, she sniffed when she saw it.

Sniffed. Is it any wonder I hated the bitch?

So I was pretty fucking shocked to find that her home was basically a wreck. Clothing was piled up all over, her little knickknacks were spread out on the floor. It almost looked like there *had* been zombie activity here, except that there wasn't any telltale blood or sludge.

Gina shut the door and bolted three deadlocks in rapid succession. When she turned to us she had her "happy hostess" face on.

"Can I get you anything to drink or eat?"

I looked around again. "Gina, is everything okay? You didn't have anyone get in here, did you?"

Her gaze swung on me, sharp and focused and angry. "What are you talking about?"

I gave Dave a helpless look. Couldn't he see how bizarre this situation was? Our eyes met and I prepared for him to give me a shrug and leave me to fight this battle on my own. In the past, when it came to his family, that was what he had done.

Not this time. To my relief, he came forward and grasped his sister's shoulders gently. "I think Sarah is just worried because your house is usually so tidy. Are you feeling all right, Gina?"

She blinked at him. "Of course. You just caught me during a chore day. If I'd known you were coming, I would have been ready. These pop-in visits are never as organized as the planned ones. You really should have called."

"The phones are down," I said softly and briefly wondered if she had Internet so I could try to reach my family again. I'd have to ask later.

She ignored me as she pulled from Dave's arms and went into the kitchen. "Now let me get you something."

While Gina bustled in the kitchen, I motioned Dave to me. We sat down on the couch together and I whispered, "This is crazy, right? She nearly killed us by shooting out the door without even looking and now she's acting like we put her out by popping in for a 'visit'."

He nodded. "It *is* weird, even for Gina."

I drew back in surprise. Dave had never even implied that his sister was...*weird*. And God help me when I did.

"Do you think she's in shock?" I asked. "She was at the parade when the zombie outbreak began in Longview. Conrad even said she was attacked. I assume she saw some shit go down and she's been alone ever since."

"Maybe we can snap her out of it." Dave said, then smiled up at her as Gina came back into the room carrying some sandwiches and diet Cokes. Even though I was worried, I couldn't help but dig in. Since the night before we left Seattle and had a frozen pizza, this was the closest thing to a real meal we'd had.

Gina watched me shovel my food down with another of her hated sniffs and then turned her attention to Dave.

"So how are you?"

He shot me a side glance. "Well, actually Gina, I'm hurt."

He set his plate aside and gingerly rolled up his pant leg. I leaned in closer to see his injury even as I guzzled my drink. Although the bruises from his fall were really ugly and the thing looked like it hurt like a son of a bitch, the swelling had thankfully gone down, lending credence to our thought about a bone bruise.

"What happened?" Gina squealed as she dropped down on the floor to get a better look.

"So much." He stared at her evenly. "During the attack, we had to run away from some bad people, Gina. And I got hurt during our escape."

"Bad people?" His sister glared at me like I was the "bad people" he was referring to and then looked back at him. "I have told you again and again that the city is no place for a decent person to live. But no, Sarah has to insist on staying there for her 'career'."

I gritted my teeth because none of that was remotely true. Seriously, she couldn't have gotten it more wrong. Oh man, did I want to say something. In the past, I would have. But I kept thinking of something Dr. Kelly had said during our therapy about respecting family boundaries.

Dave tilted his head. "Gina, this isn't about the crime level in Seattle. And it isn't about Sarah. You have to know that, don't you?"

"I'll get you an ice pack," Gina snapped as she got up and huffed off to the kitchen. When she slammed the fridge door, both Dave and I flinched.

She came back and handed the ice pack to him. He rested it on the injury with a sigh of relief and leaned closer to her. Since she didn't seem to be responding to what he'd said earlier, Dave tried something else.

"We saw Conrad, Gina. He told us you were at the parade when it was attacked."

There was a long moment's hesitation and Gina stared at Dave without blinking. Finally she whispered, "Hoodlums. Probably from Portland."

I wrinkled my brow at her utter disregard of what was happening around her. She had told herself this elaborate fairy tale and now she believed it.

"You're right that they probably came from Portland," I said slowly. "But Gina, you *had* to see that they weren't just some hoodlums come here to cause trouble. They bit people, right? They ate people. And then those people turned into things just like the other monsters."

Her gaze moved to me and narrowed. "You and your foolish thoughts, Sarah. Seriously, you're describing something out of a horror movie. I know the radio and television ramble on...but-but they've got it wrong. This is just some roving gang meant to scare us, meant to—"

Dave slammed his palm against the coffee table and both Gina and I jumped. I've known my husband a long time and I've never seen him do something like that. Nor had I ever heard the take-charge tone he took next.

"Gina, snap the fuck out of it. This isn't a game, this isn't a gang and it isn't some whacked out crime spree you've got in your head from watching too much *CSI* and *Murder, She Wrote* reruns."

He made a grab for her hands and she gasped as he took them.

"There has been an outbreak of some kind of infection," he said slowly, like he was trying to explain this to someone too young or confused to understand. "When an infected person bites another, it turns them into a monster. A zombie, for lack of a better term. You have to accept that."

"David—" She pulled her hands away and started to clear the plates, but he shoved them away and grabbed her again, yanking her down on the chair.

"God damn it, Gina. Tell me you understand what I'm saying. It could mean the difference between life and death."

She stared at him and her eyes started to fill with tears. I couldn't believe what I was seeing. For years I'd been telling Dave he needed to stop being the youngest kid in his family and start acting like an adult when he was around them. We fought about that almost every time we visited Gina or his parents.

And now he was doing it. He wasn't Gina's baby brother or the golden youngest child of his family at that moment. He was a man taking charge in a bad situation.

Is it wrong that I kind of wanted to send Gina to the store and jump his bones? Yes?

Well, what can you do?

Gina's face crumpled. "I saw them do things..." she started, her hands beginning to shake. "People I knew, people who have been my neighbors...parents of the kids I teach at the school...David, they *changed* and started trying to kill people. If Conrad hadn't grabbed me—"

She broke off and David put his arms around her as she pretty much collapsed, sobbing into his shoulder as he smoothed her hair gently.

"It's okay. It's going to be okay."

He looked at me over the top of her head. We both knew it might not be okay. In fact, after everything we'd all been through, I think we'd guarantee it in some way. Nothing would be the same, that was for sure.

But Gina needed to hear it. And I think David needed to say it.

She pulled back and he patted her hand gently. "I'll get you some tea, okay?"

I tensed as he got to his feet and moved toward the kitchen, his walk stiff and slow. Shit, he was going to leave me alone with her. She looked at me as she sank back into the chair and I tried to smile.

"I can imagine it's been tough," I said. "Especially since you've been here alone."

She nodded slowly and I could see she was thinking about whatever had happened that she hadn't yet shared. "The last couple of days have been scary. Conrad came to check on me a few times, though. That was nice."

I tilted my head as I looked at her. Huh. The way she smiled when she said Conrad's name was a little... *unexpected*. I wouldn't have thought he was her type, really. Martha Stewart and... um... I guess, Jeff Foxworthy? An odd couple, but I smiled at her.

"He was the one who told us you were okay. He's coming by later to check on us."

Her eyes brightened a little and her hand fluttered up to smooth her hair in another telltale reaction. "That will be nice."

The silence set in. Gina and I had never had very much to talk about, really. We were different and you know we never liked each other. For a long time we just sat, staring at each other.

I fought for something to say to her, but I couldn't think of a damned thing. Finally, she was the one to break the silence.

"So I guess you guys saw a lot, too? Coming from Seattle, I mean."

I thought about everything that had happened for the past three days and shook my head. She didn't look at me. I don't think she really wanted to hear it all any more than I wanted to say it out loud, so I just whispered, "So much, Gina, it would take me a year to explain it all."

Before she could respond, David came back into the

room with two cups of tea. He set them down in front of each of us and then took a place beside me.

"Okay, so now we're here and we've all acknowledged what's going on," he said as he put the ice pack back on his leg and propped it up on the table with a sigh. "So the next step is where to go now."

Gina had been sipping her tea, but she choked on it as she stared at her brother. "Go? What do you mean where to *go* now? I'm not going anywhere."

Dave and I exchanged another look at her resistance.

"This place isn't safe," Dave explained with the patience of a saint. "You're too isolated and with so many people here turned to zombies—"

"I don't want to leave," she snapped. "It's not safe out there. It wasn't safe before, but now there are zombies or the infected or whatever you want to call them. We just have to wait until the government—"

"According to some people, the government is burning down cities where the infection is located," I interrupted, searching for something, anything to say that would make her get what was happening. "What's to say they won't come here? That they won't decide to wipe out the entire West Coast if they think it will stop this?"

She blinked at me. "Burning?"

Her brother nodded. "Yes."

I swallowed. "And Gina, I have family around here, too. My Dad is just down in San Diego and I haven't been able to talk to him since this started except for one e-mail the first day. Do you want me to abandon him? To just forget about him?"

A tear slid down my cheek and I wiped it away in surprise. When I first brought up the subject, I admit it was to manipulate her into agreeing to go with us, but I realized now that it went deeper than that.

Just like every good little girl, in that moment I wanted my Daddy.

"No," Gina whispered and for the first time maybe ever her expression was soft as she looked at me. "Of course you can't just forget about your father. My laptop is here, do you want to look?"

My heart swelled as she motioned to the dining room table where her laptop rested. "Can I?"

"Of course!"

I rushed over and flipped the top up. The machine blinked to life from its sleep mode and I hurriedly entered in the address to access my e-mail from the Internet. As the little hourglass rolled in the corner, I prayed. Prayed I could connect, prayed I'd have some kind of message from my Dad.

Finally, the page loaded. "Fuck," I muttered as I scrolled down the line of messages. "God damned SPAM, now isn't the time to increase my penis size."

"There's never a wrong time to get a bigger penis," David said with a quiet chuckle as he came to stand behind me. His hand settled on my shoulder and I appreciated the comfort of his touch more than ever.

"There!" I gasped as I saw the new message from my father. I clicked it and it opened. As always, since my Dad wasn't a man to write a page when three lines would suffice, it was short and sweet.

City overrun. Heard Chicago might be free of infestation. Be careful, love you.

I stared at the thirteen words. Maybe the last ones I'd ever have from my dad.

"He's gone," I murmured. "He had to run."

Gina got up. "I'm sorry." She actually sounded like it, too.

David cupped my chin and turned my face toward his. "He's tough and he's smart. He was in 'Nam, for God's sake. He'll be okay."

I nodded. I believed it, actually. My Dad was the toughest guy I knew. If anyone would survive, it was him.

"And he says there might be safety in the Midwest," David said as he turned toward his sister and back to our problem at hand. Her reluctance to even consider leaving might get us all killed. "And that's all the more reason to think about leaving this place."

Gina swallowed hard, but then she jerked out a nod.

"Now maybe we don't have to leave today," Dave continued, "But we've got to face facts that at some point we're going to have to run. So why don't we make some dinner and see if we can figure out how to do it with the least chance at zombie infection?"

Gina and I stared at my suddenly take-charge husband and we both nodded at once. It was the beginnings of a plan starting to take shape. And right now a plan was the best thing we had.

CHAPTER 25

Hang out with other couples. It will remind you
how lucky you are not to be a zombie.

We had almost finished making dinner when the power
went out.

"It must be a fuse," Gina said brightly as she turned
away from the still-glowing gas range top.

"I don't think so," Dave said, his voice flat and filled
with concern as he looked around the dark room for a
flashlight or a candle.

He finally found it and I shivered as the bright globe lit
up and filled the dim kitchen with a sickly glow.

My voice cracked as I whispered, "They turned off
the lights."

He nodded as Gina started to light some candles.

"Yeah. Or whoever was supposed to keep them on
is…" He didn't have to finish the sentence, so instead he
smiled at Gina. "Hey, I'll check the fuse box, though. It
can't hurt. Basement, right?"

She nodded, but her frown remained long and drawn
and her face worried as she looked at him. Taking the

flashlight and a shotgun, David left the kitchen and with a brief smile toward Gina, I went back to tending the chicken breasts cooking on the stove.

I guess I did it for her sake, but also for my own. As many zombie fights as David and I had been in together, him going into the basement made me nervous. His injury slowed him down and in the dark...

Well, I didn't want to think about it.

And I didn't have to for long, because Dave hadn't been gone for five minutes when there was a banging at the front door. I jumped and turned toward Gina.

"That's probably Conrad," she said as she pushed off from the counter and moved toward the living room. "I'm glad he made it in time for dinner."

I grabbed her arm before she could get too far.

"No," I whispered. "Let me. You stay here."

I took the handgun that was on the kitchen table and slid toward the front door like I'd always seen people do it on *Law and Order* and about a billion other cop shows and movies. When I reached the door, I rose up on my tiptoes to look out the peephole and sighed with relief.

"Conrad," I said on a sigh as I opened the door. "Hi!"

He smiled as he wiped his feet on the mat outside, which was still covered in broken glass from earlier in the day, though he didn't remark about it. With a sigh, he stepped inside. This close, he looked tired, but after a day of patrolling for zombies, it didn't surprise me.

"Looks like you found her all right," he said.

"We did," I said. "Thank you so much for your help. We're making some supper before we figure out what to do next. Will you join us? It looks like you've earned a good meal and some company."

He hesitated but then he nodded. "W-Well, I can't see the harm." He looked around. "Looks like they finally cut the power, huh?"

I nodded. "Yes, Dave went down to check the breaker, but I think we all know it's not that. I'll go down and get him. Gina's still in the kitchen, I'm sure she'll be happy to see you."

He hesitated again and I frowned. Maybe he didn't like Gina as much as she liked him or something. But this was the least of our problems, and one they'd just have to work out on their own, so I ignored it and headed down to the basement.

"Dave," I called out at the top. "I'm coming down. It's me so don't shoot, okay?"

His voice came from the back of the dark area. "Gotcha. I'm in the back. The breaker's fine, not that it's a surprise."

I made my way through the darkness toward the dim glow of his flashlight. He was still staring at the fuses as if he could somehow magically make them flow with electricity again.

"So they *did* cut the power," I sighed when I reached his side.

He nodded. "Yeah. But we knew they would eventually. I'm surprised we lasted what…three days?"

I changed the subject because the power situation was too upsetting. "Conrad got here."

"Oh yeah?" he asked, distracted as he handed me the flashlight and closed the circuit breaker box.

"I figured I'd give him a minute alone with Gina."

He turned toward me with a blank expression. "Why would you do that?"

"She likes him, dummy." I laughed.

He stared even harder and I swear I could see the question mark appear in a cartoon bubble above his head. "Bullshit."

"No bullshit. She likes him." I looked toward the upstairs area. There wasn't much light, just a dim flicker from the candles and lanterns Gina had lit. "But I'm not sure he feels the same. Still, we should offer to take him with us when we go."

"Why wouldn't he like her? And why would she like him?" he asked, his voice still filled with blank disbelief.

I laughed as we started for the stairs. "Because that's what people do, babe. Even in these circumstances. Conrad is a good shot and he has some skill with cars. He'll come in handy. Just don't go all 'caveman must protect sister' on him, okay? He's a good guy. She could do way worse."

We got to the top of the stairs and in the increased light I saw Dave's scowl.

"Okay, bad boy," I teased. "Why don't you just stay here then and cool down? I'll break up the lovebirds and then we'll eat."

He shrugged. "Fine. But send Conrad in here, huh?"

I looked at him. Actually this protective streak was kind of cute, not that I thought Gina needed it. Still, I nodded as I went into the kitchen.

I stopped almost immediately because what I saw proved exactly what I'd been saying to David and what I'd suspected earlier.

Gina was standing in front of the sink and Conrad was standing before her. He was pressed up against her and from the angle I was at, it looked like they were kissing.

I smothered a smile. Well, Dave was just going to have to get over that. I cleared my throat, but the lovers didn't break apart. Under normal circumstances I might have walked away and given them a minute, but we had a lot to discuss and I wasn't sure Dave wouldn't come charging in if he knew his precious sister was making out with a random guy.

"Hey, Conrad?" I said, this time louder.

He lifted his head from hers and then slowly turned. To my utter horror, his mouth was covered in blood and his red eyes glowed in the candles.

"Oh fuck!" I screamed. "Dave!!"

I could hear him coming, but Conrad was already heading across the kitchen. I couldn't get my gun out of my waist fast enough, so I grabbed for the closest thing. The frying pan off the stove. Normally it would have burned me, but of course Gina had put a little cozy around the metal handle to keep it from being dangerous. As I picked it up, I briefly wondered if she'd crocheted the thing herself.

But that thought left my mind as Conrad lunged for me. I swung, connecting with the pan right across his temple. Hot grease flowed onto his flesh, burning part of his cheek away. He growled and went for me again. I slammed the heavy, cast iron frying pan a second time, sending him flying backward.

I jumped on top of him, crushing the frying pan down against his skull over and over until there was no chance of him coming back to life because he had no head left.

I stood up, tossing the bloody pan away as I stared at the now nearly headless body.

"Oh no," Dave whispered from behind me.

I spun around. Dave had stopped and was now standing at the kitchen entrance, staring at Gina. She had slumped to the floor when Conrad released her and blood was spurting merrily from the fresh bite mark on her shoulder.

"Oh no," I repeated the sentiment as we both went for her at the same time.

Dave fell to the ground and swept her up, holding her in his arms as I got down on my knees before them and checked the wound. Already the flesh where Conrad's teeth had closed was beginning to gray and ooze blackness.

"Oh shit," I whispered. "Dave..."

He shook his head at me, denying what my tone implied. Tears filled his eyes. "No. No, Gina. You listen to me, you're okay."

She looked up at him. "David?"

He nodded. "Yes, Gin, it's me. I've got you. We're going to fix you up."

She shook her head. "Oh honey, no. You know better."

He turned his gaze on me. "Why did you let him in? Why didn't you check?"

I would have flinched if his tone wasn't so pained and not angry. Plus, I was asking myself the same question. Over and over again as I began to remember all the signs Conrad had given that something wasn't exactly right.

"I'm sorry," I moaned. "Oh Gina, I'm so sorry."

She turned toward me and I waited for her to accuse me of doing this on purpose. But instead she whispered, "No, there was no reason to think.... He seemed so fine.

He seemed so normal. We were talking and then he had me against the sink. He kissed me. He said, 'I'm sorry, darlin'. I thought he was apologizing for kissing me but..."

She trailed off with a great shudder. "I can feel it changing inside of me already. I don't want to change."

Dave held her tighter. "You won't. You'll be okay."

Gina shook her head. "I won't, honey, And there's only one way to end this before I'm gone forever and won't be able to control myself."

Dave's fingers tightened from where he held her and his face went almost as gray as a zombie's. I could see he was thinking about Amanda and all the other "acquaintances" we'd been forced to slay in the last few days.

But this was different. This wasn't some unimportant person on the outer fringes of our lives. This was family.

"Gina..." His voice cracked as he whispered her name.

She smiled at him, loving and like a parent rather than a sister. Before that had annoyed me but now I appreciated it a lot more.

Her gaze shifted to me, slightly unfocused and soft. "Sarah... *you* have to do it."

I drew back as I realized what she was asking me. "Oh God, Gina—"

She coughed and a bit of black phlegm covered her bottom lip. "You and I never got along, but I believe with all my heart that you love Davy. You would do anything to protect him. And a brother shouldn't have to kill his sister."

Tears trickled down my cheeks. She was right, of course. "Okay. I'll do it."

Dave turned on me. "Sarah!"

"Look at me," Gina whispered, her voice starting to change. "You give me a hug. And then you go out of the room. You let Sarah take care of you. Let *me* take care of you this one last time."

He tensed and I thought he'd argue. But I guess he could see as well as we could that this was over. In a few minutes, Gina would be gone, replaced by a monster he'd never forget if he didn't walk away now.

"I love you," he whispered as he hugged her.

Then he got up with a wince of pain, both physical and emotional. I rose with him and squeezed his hand before I let him limp from the room with silent tears streaming down his haggard face.

I looked down at Gina as I withdrew the handgun from my waistband. My hands shook as I lifted it and aimed for her, but I couldn't bring myself to depress the trigger.

"I don't know if I can do it," I whispered, my voice breaking. "Gina—"

She smiled at me in a way she never had before. With real warmth. With real emotion. And in that moment, I realized why Dave loved her so much. And how much we were both about to lose.

"Honey, you're doing the right thing," she choked. "Now you do that and then you go take care of Dave. You two keep running. But run together. Stay together. Find more family and stay together."

I smiled through my tears. "We will. We will, I promise you."

I lifted the gun again. "Now close your eyes, Gina. Just close your eyes."

"I love you, Sarah," she whispered as her eyes, still so much like David's even though they were starting to tint red, fluttered shut.

"I love you, too," I sobbed.

And then I pulled the trigger.

CHAPTER 26

Love one another. Zombie infestation or not, it's the only thing that matters in the end.

The next morning we buried Gina on the hill behind her house under a tree.

It took quite a bit of time to convince David to do it, but we buried Conrad beside her. In the end I just kept reminding him of how good a man Conrad had been when he was alive. And how the *thing* that attacked his sister wasn't really the same man who had lived next door to her for years.

We stood in front of the markers we had fashioned from some wood we found in the barn that day, and I have to say even Gina would have approved of the Martha Stewart job I'd done on hers. I'd carved her name so carefully and decorated it with fabric and flowers. Sure, those things would fade, but they were beautiful now and somehow that mattered in the midst of everything ugly around us.

Slowly I put my arm around my husband and looked up at him in the bright sunshine.

"Do you hate me?" I asked.

We hadn't talked about what I'd done since the night before. Once I'd shot Gina, I'd just come into the living room. He'd been sitting waiting for me, his head in his hands, and we'd cried together for a long time.

Then we'd gone to bed and I'd risen long before him to tidy up the bodies for the burial.

He looked at me and there was shock on his face, as if he hadn't ever thought of such a thing. I was relieved even before he spoke.

"Of course not. We both know... we *all* knew she was going to change and it would have been so much worse. I love you for doing it, I don't think I could have." He hesitated. "Do you think I should have?"

"No," I whispered. "That's too much to ask of any brother. You just remember her the way she was before, when you were kids. That's the best thing you can do."

He nodded. "I'm trying so hard to do that, Sarah. I hope I can someday."

We were quiet for a while, just looking at the graves as a soft late summer breeze made the leaves shiver on the tree above us. We hadn't seen any zombies this far out of town all day, so it almost felt *normal* here in that moment.

"You know what she told me?" I said after a while.

He looked at me. "What?"

"That we should stay together." I smiled at him. "So what do you think, babe? Are we going to stay together?"

He nodded without even an ounce of hesitation. "Hell, yeah we're going to stay together. Is there even a question?"

"No. Not anymore," I said and meant it for the first time in a long time.

"So what do we do?" he asked. "I mean, we were coming here for Gina, so what do we do next?"

I smiled. "Well, since we know my Dad is out of San Diego, and that the city is already overrun, there's no point in heading South."

David nodded slowly. "Too bad, the weather would have been nice."

I chuckled. "Yeah, we could have worked on our tans while battling the zombie horde. Oh well."

"So do we go toward Chicago and hope your Dad was right about there being safety there?" Dave asked.

I thought about it a long time. I couldn't picture a way that there could be true safety left in the world. But I didn't want to give up hope completely.

"It may be our only option," I admitted. "Though I think it's going to take us a *long* time to get there."

"You're probably right. But I'm in this for the long haul, remember."

As I squeezed his hand, Dave looked down at Gina's grave and then blew a soft kiss before we started down the hill toward the house, arm in arm.

"You know, Dr. Kelly once told us that we should find a common goal to work on together," he said. "That it would bring us closer together and help us remember why we wanted to be together in the first place."

I nodded. "I think that was one of her better pieces of advice. We definitely did that over the last few days and look how strong we are now."

"Well, I think we should take it a step further. If it's going to take us weeks, maybe even months to get where we're going, what do you think about starting a business with me in the meantime?"

I stared at him. Was he serious? I mean, there were hardly any people left that I could see. I had no idea what he could be talking about.

"What kind of business? Make scented candles? Flip houses? Sell insurance?" I laughed.

"How about exterminators?" he asked as he raised an eyebrow toward me. "We joked about it, but I bet we could use our skills to help a lot of survivors who are hiding out and waiting for a government that just might not come."

I thought about it for a minute. He was right in a lot of ways. We were fucking *good* at this. And it beat slogging at my day job, anyway.

"S and D Zombie Extermination," he continued. "We take care of your undead issues."

"Zombiebusters. I like it," I laughed as we went back into Gina's house to gather up supplies.

There isn't much good to say about the zombie infestation. A lot of people died in those first few days and a lot more were still going to die before the whole thing worked itself out. Plus, don't even get me started on the mad scientists and washed-up rock stars we'd have to deal with eventually.

But I have to say, the zombie plague saved my marriage. And if you follow the rules, have each other's backs and stick together...it could save yours, too.

ACKNOWLEDGMENTS

What an odd and interesting journey this book has been for me and I'm so pleased to see it reach shelves. But without the following people, it never would have happened. First, I must thank Josh and Drea Fecht, who took us to the movies one fateful night and set off a spark in my imagination. You are wonderful friends and we're lucky to know you. I must also thank my brother and sister-in-law, Bill and Melissa Cerise-Bullock. When I asked if you wanted to run a cult, you said yes without hesitation. I'm not sure whether to be worried by that or not, but I do appreciate the unbridled enthusiasm.

I must also thank my wonderful agent, Miriam Kriss. You not only kept me going through a tough year, but you read the first thirty pages of this book and told me to finish it. Your enthusiasm for me and my work, not to mention your friendship, is a rare and wonderful thing. I also can't forget Devi Pillai and the entire team at Orbit for jumping on this project with such passion and taking it to publication. You guys rock!

Finally, I have to thank my husband, Michael. You are my rock, and I fully trust that you would get me out of a zombie outbreak alive, even though I'd probably drive you crazy the entire time. I love you.

extras

POCKET
BOOKS

meet the author

A Facebook application once told **Jesse Petersen** that she'd only survive a day in a zombie outbreak, but she doesn't believe that. For one, she's a good shot and two, she has an aversion to bodily fluids, so she'd never go digging around in zombie goo. Until the zombie apocalypse, she lives in the Midwest with her husband and two cats.

Find out more about the author at
http://www.jessepetersen.net.

interview

Greetings everyone, this is your on-the-ground zombie apocalypse reporter Zanderson Snooper. I'm coming to you today from one of the makeshift camps that have been set up all through the West Coast for survivors who are passing through. You've probably seen my Emmy-winning reports and read my Pulitzer Prize-winning articles on the subject. Anyway, today I'm lucky enough to get an exclusive interview with some of the few survivors of this summer's zombie outbreak in Seattle. I'm here with Sarah and David (who have refused to give their last name) to get the real scoop on zombies, marriage, and what it means when you kill everyone you know.

Zanderson: Thanks for joining us.

Sarah: You gave us Diet Coke and ammo, how could we refuse?

Zanderson: Well, anything to help the cause. You two escaped Seattle, didn't you? That was the front line of the attack. Can you tell us where you were when you knew the zombies were attacking?

David: We come from Seattle, yes, and you reporters tell us that the zombies escaped from a lab at the University of Washington, so I guess you could tell people more about that. As for where we were, that's really none of your damned business.

Zanderson: You're so defensive, David. Is that because you two were in a marriage counseling session when you first encountered zombies?

Sarah: How the hell does he know that? How the hell do you know that?

Zanderson: A reporter does his homework and the people have a right to know!

Sarah: Look, jagoff, yeah. We were in marriage counseling, okay?

David: Shit, Sarah, just spill your guts. Do you want to tell him about our sex life, too?

Zanderson: You could.

Sarah: Maybe another time, you are kind of cute, you silver fox.

David: Sarah!

Sarah: Um, I saw you look at the tits on the zombie strippers we killed. Cut me some slack. The point is, the way we found out about the apocalypse is because we caught our marriage counselor eating the people who had the appointment before ours. We killed her, end of subject.

Zanderson: You don't seem to feel very badly about it.

David: She was ripping us off. Our marriage did a lot better once she was dead.

Sarah: Oh, don't say that. I mean, some of her advice did come in very useful when we were getting out of the city. We used a lot of what she told us, as well as what we read in books about saving our marriage, so it wasn't a complete waste.... We did have to kill her, though. These things happen.

Zanderson: So you used marriage counseling to survive the zombie outbreak, but you also claim to have used zombie movies as a way to stay alive. Any movies in particular my readers should check out?

Sarah: Sure. In order to survive a zombie apocalypse, fill up your Netflix queue with some of the following: *Shaun of the Dead*, *Zombieland*, *Dawn of the Dead*, anything with *Resident Evil* in the title, um...

David: Don't forget *Scooby-Doo on Zombie Island*.

Sarah: What?

Zanderson: What???

David: Um, it was *helpful.*

Sarah: They *do* drive a van. A van is a great vehicle for zombie highways. Plus they had snacks and I'm pretty sure Shaggy was doing medical marijuana, which I bet would be useful to have in this situation. I guess you're right.

Zanderson: Are you two done? We're getting off topic here.

David: I don't think so. You're trying to tell people how to survive a zombie attack. That's how you do it. Creative thinking, marriage counseling, and movies.

Sarah: It's a trifecta.

Zanderson: How does killing friends and family play into that trifecta?

Sarah: You're cute, but you're kind of an asshole.

David: I still don't see cute. He's got white hair, for God's sake. Are you an albino?

Zanderson: Answer the question.

David: Sure, we killed a lot of people we know. Therapists...

Sarah: Friends.

David: Family, which really sucks. But when the going gets zombie, the tough get to using their shotguns. If they don't, they die.

Sarah: Speaking of which, Zanderson, it's more than your hair that's gray. *You* wouldn't happen to be a zombie, would you?

Zanderson: Er, I think this interview is over.

Sarah: That's what I thought. We're off to massacre some zombies. Later.

introducing

If you enjoyed MARRIED WITH ZOMBIES,

look out for

FLIP THIS ZOMBIE

Book 2 of Living with the Dead

by Jesse Petersen

When the zombie plague struck, I was just an office schlub. You know the type. I was a coffee-fetching, doing-the-work-and-getting-no-credit, screamed-at-by-suits kind of girl who hated every damn second of her dead-end job. Well, I still have a dead-end job...*undead* end, I guess is more accurate. And instead of working for the man, I work for myself. So I guess the lesson is that if you find work that's meaningful, that you love, you can start your own business and make it successful.

So what's my job?

Zombiebusters Extermination, Inc. at your service. My husband David suggested we add the "Inc." to make it seem more professional. I guess in the old days we would have had a website and all that, too, but now none of that exists anymore, at least not in the badlands where the zombies still roam free.

I have to say, I liked being in business for myself and I liked working with my husband as my partner. The zombie apocalypse had been great for our marriage, and since we'd escaped Seattle a few months before, we'd been doing great.

But that isn't to say the whole "not working for the man" thing didn't have its disadvantages. Which is something we were discussing as we drove down a lonely stretch of dusty highway in Arizona. Why Arizona? Well, it was November and fucking freezing anywhere else. So we did what old people did and snowbirded our asses down south. I figured when the weather got better up North, we'd figure out what to do next.

"Why did we take another job from Jimmy?" Dave asked with annoyance lacing his voice.

I looked up from the business book I was reading. We'd looted it and about twenty more from a bookstore a few weeks back. I was all about making this work, you see. Someday, I would be the Donald Trump or Bill Gates of zombie killing.

"Um, we took a job from Jimmy because he pays," I said.

Dave shot me a side glance that was filled with incredulity. "Not well. Last time I think he gave us a six-pack, and we killed three zombies for his chicken-ass."

I laughed. "Hey, that's two brews per zombie."

Dave didn't even smile. "He has a lot of stockpile in his basement, I know he does. This time before we start, we should tell that asshole we want payment up front. Medical supplies and some canned goods."

I tossed my book in the back of the van. Oh, didn't I mention it? We drive a van. Dave likes to call it the Mystery Machine because it's totally circa 1975, but it runs like a gem and is heavy enough to do some push work when needed. Plus, I had *way* too much fun painting "Zombiebusters Exterminators, Inc." on the side and "Who Ya Gonna Call?" on the back.

That one always gets a chuckle since there's no way to call anyone anymore. If people want us, they have to post notes in the survivor camps and we go looking for them. Trust me, sometimes by the time we've gotten to a job, there hasn't been anyone left to pay us. I always feel kind of badly about that, but seriously, if you haven't figured out how to protect yourself after three months of zombie hell...well, you sort of deserve what you get.

"Look, you're the muscle in this operation," I said as I settled back in my seat and slung my booted feet onto the dash. As I flicked a little piece of brains left over from our last job from the toe, I continued, "If you want to strong-arm the guy up front, be my guest."

We were approaching our destination now and Dave slowly maneuvered the vehicle off the highway into the area of what was once southern Phoenix. There were signs of zombie activity everywhere here, both from the initial outbreak in the city and recently. Black sludge pooled in the gutters and blood streaked the walls of buildings. It was all so commonplace to us, we didn't really see it anymore. Nor did we flinch when a single zombie stepped into a crosswalk ahead of us.

He lurched forward, his right hand missing and his arm on the same side waving in a disconnected way as he moved. He had fresh blood on his chin and he grunted and groaned loudly enough that we could hear him even with the windows partly up.

We watched him make his slow cross for a bit, both of us staring with bored disinterest. Then Dave gunned the engine.

The sound made the zombie turn and he stared at us with blank, dead, red eyes that never quite focused. Still, he recognized the potential for food and he let out a roar.

Dave floored the van at the same time the zombie started a half-assed jog toward us. We collided mid-intersection and the zombie, gooey and rotting, took the brunt of the impact. His skin split, sending gore and guts flying from the seams of his torn clothing. He lay half-wrapped around our bumper, staring up at us as he squealed and clawed, even though his lower body was probably gone.

"Want me to take care of that?" I asked as I reached in the back for an axe.

"Naw," Dave said. He changed gears and rolled back in reverse. The zombie fell backward and disappeared from view until my husband got far enough away. Sure enough, his lower half was gone, split off from the initial impact.

Dave lined up the wheel of the van and rolled forward again. He didn't stop until we felt the satisfying rock of hitting the zombie skull and popping it like a melon.

Once that was done, Dave put the van in neutral and

looked at me. "So if I'm the muscle of the operation," he said, returning to our earlier conversation, "what does that make you?"

"Silly," I laughed. "I'm the brains, of course. And the beauty."

I fluffed my hair and he laughed as he threw the van in gear and we roared toward our first job of the week.